This Book
Belongs
to

The Magical Mimics in Oz

ISBN: 1620890089
ISBN-13: 978-1-62089-008-0

Dear Reader,

The *Magical Mimics in Oz* is often seen as the darkest, most frightening novel in the 40-book Oz canon. And rightly so considering the entire populace of the Emerald City, timeless Oz characters and all, fall victim to hordes of vicious shape-shifting body-snatchers.

The Retrofit story in this release, *Tote's Blemished Blossom*, is the middle of the three—both in the canonical series and in the time-line of events in the new Retrofit lore—but it was actually written last. This presented some interesting creative challenges but ultimately led to a much better overall story arc. I chose to release *The Silver Princess in Oz* and *The Shaggy Man of Oz* first simply because they were two of the rarest, least available novels in the canon.

This will most likely be the last Empty-Grave Retrofit of a canonical Oz novel since many of the others have already been digitally preserved or are the responsibility of the current copyright holders. However, if readers really enjoy the Yot stories and there is a demand for more, I may consider doing another Retrofit book after the culminating original novel *Asper and the Unheard Heroes in Oz* is released in 2013.

My goal is to provide availability, accessibility, and a bit of exciting new content for current and—more importantly—future generations of Oz fans and readers. I hope you enjoy reading about Tote, Raynaud Whitefinger, Yot, and company as much as I enjoyed writing about them.

Visit oz.empty-grave.com for updates on Empty-Grave's Oz endeavors or to provide feedback. I thank you for reading.

Adam Nicolai
Empty-Grave Publishing

empty-grave.com - website
facebook.com/pages/empty-grave-publishing/114806311932977 - facebook
twitter.com/emptygravepub - twitter feedback@empty-grave.com - comments, concerns, contact

STRAIGHT FOR THE MOUNTAIN FLEW THE BIRDS

THE
MAGICAL
MIMICS
IN

BY **JACK SNOW**, FOUNDED ON AND CONTINUING
THE FAMOUS OZ STORIES BY **L. FRANK BAUM**
ILLUSTRATED BY FRANK KRAMER

Empty-Grave Publishing
www.empty-grave.com

This Book is Dedicated to
My Mother
Roselyn Hyde Snow

".... to please a child is
a sweet and lovely thing
that warms one's heart and
brings its own reward."
—L. FRANK BAUM.

TO THE CHILDREN

As long as I can remember, I have been reading Oz books, and now I am very proud and happy to have been permitted to write a book about the latest happenings in the Land of Oz.

Mr. Kramer has made many delightful illustrations for this book, and I know you will enjoy the fun and life that he has so skillfully put into his pictures.

As for the Magical Mimics, I think you will agree with me that these surprising creatures made things pretty exciting for our Oz friends while they were in the Emerald City. Nevertheless, now that the Mimics are powerless. I am inclined to forgive them; since, had it not been for them, Dorothy, and the Wizard would not have discovered winsome little Ozana and her Story Blossom Garden.

I hope this story pleases you and that you will write me many letters—all of which I promise to answer as soon as possible. I am sure that your suggestions and ideas will be of great help to me in writing future Oz books, and I am looking forward with much pleasure to receiving them.

JACK SNOW

January 10, 1946

CHAPTER 1

Toto Carries a Message

oto," called Princess Ozma of Oz, as a small black dog trotted down the corridor past the open door of her study in the Royal Palace of the Emerald City, "Toto, will you do me a favor?"

"Certainly," answered the little dog, his bright eyes regarding the Princess questioningly. "What can I do for your Majesty?"

Ozma smiled. "I wonder if you would go to Dorothy's rooms and ask her to join me here as soon as possible."

"That'll be easy, Ozma," said Toto, "I was just on my way to see Dorothy. It's time for our morning romp in the garden."

Toto Carries a Message

"Well," laughed Ozma, "I shall keep Dorothy for only a few minutes, then she can join you in the garden for your play."

"Thank you, Ozma," replied Toto as he turned and trotted down the corridor leading to Dorothy's suite of rooms.

As the little dog disappeared, the smile slowly faded from Ozma's face, and the lovely little ruler of the world's most beautiful fairyland looked unusually serious.

The truth was that Ozma was thinking of events that had happened many years before in the history of the Land of Oz. Not always had Oz been a fairy realm. In those olden times Oz had been nothing more than a remarkably beautiful country of rolling plains, wooded hills and rich farm lands. Indeed, Oz had not been so much different from our own United States, except that it was surrounded on all sides by a Deadly Desert. It was this desert which prevented curious men from the great outside world from finding their way to Oz. For the fumes and gases that rose from the shifting sands of the desert were deadly poison to all living things, and for a human to have set foot on the desert would have meant instant and terrible death. Consequently, all living things avoided the Deadly Desert, and it is no wonder that Oz was so entirely secluded and went unnoticed by the rest of the world for so many long years.

Meanwhile, the Oz people were happy and contented, living their simple carefree lives without worries or troubles. The soil of Oz was fertile and the people were naturally industrious, so there was always an abundance of everything for everyone. Hence destructive and terrible wars were unknown in Oz even in the olden days.

Toto Carries a Message

One fine day Queen Lurline, Ruler of all the fairies in the world, chanced to be flying over the Land of Oz with her fairy band. She was greatly impressed with the beauty of the hidden country. The Fairy Queen paused, flying in wide circles over the peaceful land. Here was a country so entirely beautiful and charming that it deserved to be a fairy realm.

Queen Lurline sought out the King of this favored land and found him to be an old man with no son or daughter to whom he could pass on his crown. With great joy the old King accepted the tiny, baby fairy whom Queen Lurline placed in his care. When the baby fairy attained her full age of girlhood (no fairy ever appears to be older than a young girl of fourteen or fifteen) she was to be crowned Princess Ozma of Oz.

From the time of Lurline's visit, Oz became a fairyland, abounding in enchantments and strange happenings. Indeed, several of the inhabitants of Oz fell to studying the magic arts and became witches and magicians, very nearly preventing Ozma from becoming the rightful ruler of the fairyland.

Ozma was fully aware that she was a member of Queen Lurline's fairy band, and she was justly proud of her immortal heritage. She knew, too, that she owed allegiance to the powerful Fairy Queen, and that was the reason she appeared so thoughtful this morning as she awaited Princess Dorothy.

Ozma's reverie was broken by a gentle rap on the open door. Looking up, she saw Dorothy standing in the doorway.

"Come in, my dear," said Ozma, "there is something I must discuss with you."

CHAPTER 2

Ozma and Glinda Go Away

What is it, Ozma?" Dorothy asked, as she sat down beside her friend.

"Dorothy," Ozma began, thoughtfully, "you have heard me tell the story of how the good Queen Lurline left me here as a baby to become the Ruler of the Land of Oz."

"Of course, Ozma, and how you were stolen by old Mombi, the witch, and—"

"Yes," interrupted Ozma, smiling, "all that is true, but the important fact is that now the day has arrived when I must answer the summons of the great Fairy Queen. You see," continued the girlish ruler seriously, "every 200 years all the members of Queen Lurline's fairy band gather for a Grand Council in the beautiful Forest of Burzee which lies just across the Deadly Desert to the South of Oz."

"Isn't that the forest where Santa Claus was found as an infant and adopted by the Forest Nymph?" asked Dorothy eagerly.

"Yes," replied Ozma, "Burzee is indeed a famous forest. For untold centuries its cool groves have been the meeting place of Queen Lurline and her subjects. They gather to discuss and plan the work they will do during the next two centuries.

"In the old days," Ozma's voice was musing and thoughtful as she continued, "when mankind was simpler and gentler of nature, it was easier for the fairies to do their good works and to aid the helpless humans. But today few humans believe in fairies."

"The children do," Dorothy suggested.

"Yes," said Ozma, "but unfortunately as the children grow older and become men and women, they forget all they ever knew about fairies. I wish," she added wistfully, "that the men and women of the world would keep a bit of their childhood with them. They would find it a valuable thing."

"When will you be going, Ozma?" Dorothy asked softly.

"Tomorrow morning," Ozma replied. "And so important is this meeting that I have asked Glinda the Good to accompany me, although she is not a member of Queen Lurline's fairy band."

"Ozma," said Dorothy seriously, her chin cupped in her hand, "there is one thing I have often wondered about. What did Queen Lurline do after she left you here to become the Ruler of Oz?"

"There is a story," Ozma began with a far-away look in her eyes, "that after she made Oz a fairyland, Queen Lurline flew away to the Land of the Phanfasms, that strange realm lying southeast of Oz, across the Deadly Desert and bordering the Kingdom of the Nomes."

"I remember the Phanfasms," Dorothy nodded.

"They are the wicked creatures who came with the Nome King through his tunnel under the Deadly Desert to conquer Oz."

"Yes, and thanks to the wisdom of our famous Scarecrow, we were able to render them harmless," Ozma recalled with a smile. "Did Queen Lurline go to see the Phanfasms after she left Oz?" asked Dorothy.

"No," replied Ozma. "It seems that instead of going to Mount Phantastico, where the Phanfasms dwell, Queen Lurline flew to the second of the twin peaks—to Mount Illuso, home of the dread Mimics."

"I don't remember hearing about the Mimics before. Just who are they, Ozma," asked Dorothy with interest.

"Not a great deal is known about them," replied Ozma seriously, "and what we do know is so unpleasant that the Mimics are avoided as a subject of conversation. They are not humans, nor are they immortals. Like the Phanfasms, to whom they are closely related, they belong to the ancient race of Erbs—creatures who inhabited the Earth long before the coming of mankind. Both the Mimics and the Phanfasms hate all humans and immortals, for they feel that mankind, aided by the immortals, has stolen the world from them."

"They don't sound very nice to me," said Dorothy with a shudder. "Why did Queen Lurline go to see such dreadful creatures?"

Ozma's voice was grave as she answered. "Queen Lurline knew that the Mimics bitterly hated all that was good and happy and just in the world. The wise Queen fully realized that now that Oz was so beautiful and favored and its people so happy and contented a fairy folk, the Mimics would lose no time in seeking to bring unhappiness to Oz. It was to prevent this, that Queen Lurline paid her visit to Mount Illuso."

"And did she succeed?" asked Dorothy.

"Yes, my dear," replied Ozma. "Queen Lurline placed a fairy spell on the Mimics to make it impossible for them to attack the inhabitants of Oz. But let's not discuss the unpleasant Mimics any further," Ozma concluded. "Thanks to good Queen Lurline we don't even have to think about the creatures. Let us return to our conversation about you."

"About me?" asked Dorothy.

"Yes," replied Ozma. "Can't you guess why I asked you to see me this particular morning?"

"Why, to tell me about the trip you and Glinda are planning," said Dorothy.

"And something more, too," continued Ozma. "Who do you think will rule the Emerald City and the Land of Oz, while both Glinda and I are absent?"

"I suppose either the Little Wizard or the Scarecrow," ventured Dorothy, remembering that in the past both the Wizard and the Scarecrow had ruled the Land of Oz.

"No," replied Ozma calmly. "You, Dorothy, will be the ruler of the Emerald City and the Land of Oz in my absence."

"Me?" cried Dorothy. "Oh, Ozma, I'm only a little girl! I don't know the first thing about ruling!"

"You are a Princess of Oz," stated Ozma with dignity. "I shall appoint the Wizard as your Counselor and Advisor. With his wisdom and your honesty of heart and sweetness of nature, I am confident the Land of Oz will be well-ruled."

Dorothy was silent, considering.

"Come, my dear," said Ozma with a smile. "I shall be gone only three short days. I am sure once you have become accustomed to the idea, you will enjoy the novel experience of being a real ruler, so do not worry."

Rising from the divan, Ozma concluded: "I must go now to inform the Courtiers and Lords and Ladies of my journey. I will instruct them in the regular affairs of state to be carried on in my absence, so that you will not be annoyed with these routine matters."

Ozma kissed Dorothy on the cheek and the two girls left the room arm in arm parting a few minutes later as

Ozma and Glinda Go Away

Ozma went about making preparations for her journey. Dorothy joined Toto who was waiting patiently for her in the lovely gardens of the Royal Palace.

The little dog quickly noticed that his mistress was not nearly so carefree in her play as usual, but seemed more serious and thoughtful. He wondered if this had anything to do with her conversation with Ozma, but since Dorothy didn't mention the subject to him and seemed to be so busy with her own thoughts, Toto, being a wise little dog, refrained from troubling her with questions.

Dorothy had a long talk with the Wizard later in the day. The little man pointed out that Dorothy's duties as a ruler would be very slight, so well-governed was Oz and so well-behaved were the Oz people. Nevertheless, Dorothy was greatly cheered and relieved when the Wizard promised to help her, should any problem arise that she found troubling.

Ozma's time was so entirely taken up with affairs of state and the many preparations for her absence from her beloved country, that Dorothy saw nothing of the girlish ruler during the remainder of the day.

* * * *

The morning of Ozma and Glinda's departure dawned bright and clear, with the sunlight shining brilliantly on the beautiful city of Emeralds.

Breakfast had been over for several hours when Glinda the Good Sorceress arrived from her castle far to the South in the Quadling Country of the Land of Oz. Glinda and Ozma went immediately to the Royal

Throne Room where the famous Oz personages waited to witness their departure.

At exactly 10 o'clock Princess Ozma seated herself in her Emerald Throne, while the stately Glinda stood at her right. Before them was as strange and impressive an assemblage of Nobles, Courtiers and old friends as ever gathered together in any fairy realm.

Among those present were: the famous Scarecrow of Oz with his highly polished companion, Nick Chopper, the nickel-plated Tin Woodman; comical Jack Pumpkinhead astride the wooden Sawhorse who was Ozma's personal steed and earliest companion; Scraps, the jolly Patchwork Girl; sweet little Trot and her faithful sailor friend, grizzled old Cap'n Bill; Betsy Bobbin and her mule, Hank; the cheerful Shaggy Man looking shaggier than ever; the Highly Magnified and Thoroughly Educated Woggle Bug wearing his wisest expression for this important occasion; the stately Cowardly Lion who was one of Dorothy's oldest friends and his companion the Hungry Tiger who longed to devour fat babies but never did because his conscience wouldn't permit him to; that strange creature the Woozy whose eyes flashed real fire when he became angry; Button Bright, the boy from Philadelphia who had been Dorothy's companion on several wonderful adventures; Ojo the Lucky and his Unc Nunkie; Dorothy's beloved Aunt Em and Uncle Henry, and of course the Little Wizard, and many, many others.

Ozma stood before her throne and raised her hand. Immediately silence settled over the assemblage in the vast Throne Room.

"As you all know," the Princess said, "Glinda and I are about to attend an important Fairy Conference in the distant Forest of Burzee. We shall be gone from Oz for a period of three days. During that time, Princess Dorothy will be your sovereign and ruler."

Ozma removed her dainty fairy wand from the folds of her gown and lifted it into the air. For a moment she smiled on all, then, with a graceful wave

of the wand and before the onlookers realized what was happening, both she and Glinda had vanished.

But Dorothy knew that even at that moment Queen Lurline was greeting the lovely Ozma and the stately Glinda in the depths of the enchanted Forest of Burzee.

CHAPTER 3
Mount Illuso

On that far away day those many years ago, when Queen Lurline had left the baby Ozma to become the ruler of Oz, Queen Lurline did not pause, for she knew the most important part of her work was still to be done. If the Land of Oz was to be the happy fairy-land she hoped it would be, she must protect it from the evil of the Mimics.

With this thought in mind, the good Queen left Oz and flew straight to the bleak land of the Phanfasms. Signaling to one of her Fairy Maidens to accompany her, Queen Lurline flew down to grim Mount Illuso, home of the dread Mimics.

Mount Illuso

Pausing at the entrance to the great hollow mountain Queen Lurline bade her fairy companion await her return. Then, taking the precaution to make herself invisible to the eyes of the Mimics, the Fairy Queen stepped into the enchanted Mountain.

The sight that met her eyes caused even the good Queen Lurline to chill and falter momentarily on the rocky ledge on which she stood. Above her rose the vast, cavernous walls of the hollow mountain. Spread out below were the corridors burrowed into the rock by the Mimics. In dark caverns deep below these corridors the monsters made their homes.

All of this scene was lighted by flaming torches set at intervals in the walls of the cavern. The torches flared deep red, casting lurid, flickering shadows and adding to the weird unreality of the scene.

As Queen Lurline gazed, the Mimics were moving through the rough-hewn corridors or flying through the air. The most unusual thing about the creatures was their strange habit of constantly changing their shapes. They shifted restlessly from one form to another. Since they were creatures of evil, the shapes they assumed were all forms of the blackest evil and dread.

Even as Queen Lurline watched, fascinated by the strange spectacle, the Mimics shifted and changed and flitted from one loathsome shape to another. A monster bird with leathery wings and a horned head dropped to the ground, and in another second assumed the squat body of a huge toad with the head of a hyena, snarling with laughter. A crawling red lizard, all of ten feet in length, turned into a giant butterfly with black wings and the body of a serpent. A great, green bat with wicked talons alighted on a ledge not far from Queen Lurline and in an instant changed to a mammoth, hairy creature with the body of a huge ape and the head of an alligator.

The good Queen shuddered in spite of herself. What she had seen had only served to strengthen her resolution to protect the Oz people for all time against the Mimics. Immediately she began weaving a powerful

incantation. In a few minutes the enchantment was completed. Queen Lurline breathed a sigh of relief, for she knew that the Mimics were now powerless to harm any of the fairy inhabitants of the Land of Oz.

Queen Lurline was well aware that the Mimics' strange habit of changing their shapes was the least of their evil characteristics. Much more dreadful was the power possessed by these creatures to steal the shapes of both mortals and immortals. A Mimic accomplished this simply by casting himself on the shadow of his victim. Instantly the Mimic arose, a perfect double in outward appearance of the person whose shadow he had stolen. As for the unfortunate victim, he fell into a spell of enchantment, unable to move or speak, but conscious of all that was taking place about him. No wonder Queen Lurline sighed with relief when she thought that

her powerful magic had made the Oz people secure against the dread evil of the Mimics!

Queen Lurline slipped from the cavern through the stone portal of Mount Illuso. For a moment she paused, breathing deeply and gratefully of the fresh air. But she must not tarry now. She still had other important work to do here. When she returned to her fairy companion, Queen Lurline gave her brief instructions concerning the important part she was to play at Mount Illuso in the coming years. Then they both spread their fairy wings and flew straight to the very summit of the hollow mount.

The Mimics Mean Mischief

On the same morning that Ozma and Glinda left the Land of Oz for the Forest of Burzee, events of equal importance were happening in Mount Illuso, home of the Mimics.

The Mimics were ruled over by two sovereigns— King Umb and Queen Ra. It is a question which was the more wicked and dangerous of this pair. King Umb was bold and brutal, while his wife, Queen Ra, was clever and cunning. Together they made a fitting combination to rule so wicked a horde as the Mimics.

On this particular morning King Umb and Queen Ra secluded themselves in a hidden cavern, deep in the underground caves that honeycombed the depths of hollow Mount Illuso. Roughly hewn from the gray rock, this cavern was circular in shape and was filled with ancient books and strange and weird implements of sorcery and enchantment. King Umb possessed little skill in magic arts, but Queen Ra was powerful in the practice of conjuring and evil incantation.

After the visit of Queen Lurline to Mount Illuso and the casting of the powerful enchantment that prevented King Umb and Queen Ra from leading their Mimic subjects in the destruction of Oz, Queen Ra had at first raged and fumed and wildly vowed vengeance on Queen Lurline and Princess Ozma. Then, as the years passed by, the evil Queen spent more and more time lurking in the secret cavern, studying the ancient sorcery of the Erbs, employing her black arts to follow events in the history of Oz and plotting the destruction of the fairyland.

Of course the Mimic King and Queen were free to lead their hordes in attacks on people of other lands, and you may wonder why they didn't forget all about Oz and content themselves with bringing misery to other countries. The reason was that the wicked King and Queen of the Mimics despised all that was good, and they could not endure the thought of the Oz people living in peace and contentment, safe from their evil-doing. So long as the Oz inhabitants remained the happiest people in all the world, King Umb and Queen Ra could derive no satisfaction in bringing misery to other less happy lands.

Queen Ra was well aware that Princess Ozma was one of the most powerful fairy rulers in existence, and that her loyal friend, Glinda the Good, was the mightiest and wisest of all sorceresses. Nevertheless, through her own dark magic, Queen Ra had recently made two important discoveries that raised her hopes so high that she believed she might be able soon to defy both Ozma and Glinda.

First, she had discovered that Ozma and Glinda were about to depart on a journey that would take them away from the Land of Oz. Second, she had learned that in one of Ozma's books of magic records in the Royal Palace of the Emerald City was written the charm that would break the spell Queen Lurline had cast on the Mimics to protect Oz!

This morning Queen Ra had assumed the shape of a huge woman—almost a giantess—with the head of a gray wolf. King Umb wore the form of a black bear with an owl head. The Queen held in her hands a circlet of dully gleaming metal. The red eyes of her wolf head gazed at it steadily, while she muttered an incantation. As the wolf-headed woman spoke, a wisp of gray mist appeared in the center of the metal ring. The mist expanded into a ball, growing denser in appearance. Next it became milky in hue, then opalescent, finally glowing as with an inner light. Slowly a scene appeared in the metal-bound ball of shimmering opal mist. While King Umb and Queen Ra watched, the Throne Room of the Royal Palace in the Emerald City grew distinct in the milky depths of the captive ball. Princess Ozma stood by her throne with Glinda the Good at her side. The lips of the little ruler were moving, forming words, although the Mimic Monarchs could distinguish no sound. Ozma was addressing her subjects. Then the girl Ruler smiled and raised her wand. In an instant both Ozma and

Glinda had vanished. The ball of glowing mist disappeared. With a clatter Queen Ra threw the metal circlet to the stone floor of the cave and triumphantly faced the owl-headed bear.

"They have gone!" she cried.

"You are positive that now is the time for us to act?" asked King Umb.

"Absolutely!" said the wolf-headed woman. "We know that one of Ozma's magic record books holds the secret of the enchantment cast on us. We know that Ozma and Glinda will be absent from Oz for three days, leaving the country and the Emerald City unprotected by their magic arts. We know that those people who have in recent years come from the great outside world to live in Oz were not inhabitants of Oz when Lurline made it a fairyland. Thus they are not protected by the enchantment she cast on us. It will be simple for us to assume the shapes of these people—of course they are mere mortals—" the Queen added with a sneer, "but even so they will serve our purpose."

"You have a plan then?" asked the owl-headed King.

The Mimics Mean Mischief

"A plan that will result in the utter destruction of Oz and the enslavement of the Oz people," asserted the Queen with grim relish.

"Listen!" the wolf-headed woman commanded. "Tonight you and I, with Styg and Ebo, will fly swiftly across the Deadly Desert to the Land of Oz. We will go directly to the Emerald City. There we will seek out the two mortals from the great outside world whose shapes will admit us to every part of the Royal Palace. My magic arts have told me that at a certain hour tomorrow morning these two mortals will be together with no one else about to witness or interfere with our deed. After we have stolen their shapes, the helpless mortals will be seized by Styg and Ebo and returned here, where they will be our prisoners. Then we will be free to search through Ozma's magic record books. As soon as we locate the magical antidote to Lurline's enchantment, we will break the spell binding our sub-

jects. By the time Ozma and Glinda return, Oz will be overrun by Mimics, and we shall be ready to give their royal highnesses a proper reception!" Queen Ra smiled wickedly as she finished this recital.

The owl eyes of King Umb had been regarding Queen Ra intently as she revealed her plan. When she had finished, an evil leer spread over the King's furry features. "Ra," said King Umb, "you are the most wicked Queen who ever ruled the Mimics!"

And that, by Mimic standards, was the highest compliment King Umb could pay his Queen.

* * * *

Several hours after midnight, King Umb and Queen Ra, followed by the two Mimics, Styg and Ebo, slipped outside the entrance of the hollow mountain. Immediately all four assumed the shapes of giant birds, black of plumage and with powerful wings. During the creatures' long flight over the Deadly Desert to Oz, they changed shapes a number of times, but always to another form of powerful bird.

As they mounted into the air and soared through the dark night over the peak of Mount Illuso, King Umb cast a backward glance toward the summit of the mountain.

"What about the Guardian?" he asked Queen Ra uneasily.

"Bah!" the giant bird that was Queen Ra croaked derisively. "Who cares about her? Let her go on dreaming over her foolish flowers and sticks of wood—that's all she has done all these years!"

CHAPTER 5

Prisoners of the Mimics

High in the top of the tallest tower of the Royal Palace was the Wizard's apartment. In this secluded spot, the little man kept his magical tools and apparatus and could work undisturbed for long hours over difficult feats of magic.

The morning after Ozma and Glinda had left, Dorothy had climbed the stair to the Wizard's quarters, and she and the Wizard were deep in a discussion of matters of state.

Two sides of the room they occupied were composed of tall French windows, rising from the floor to the ceiling and opening onto a spacious veranda. The windows were flung wide open to admit the refreshing breeze and the welcome sunlight.

Suddenly the air was filled with the flutter of powerful wings, and four large, black-plumed birds, settled on the veranda and stepped into the room.

Glancing up in surprise at this sudden interruption, the Wizard exclaimed with annoyance, "Here, what's the meaning of this intrusion?"

(Since all birds and animals in the Land of Oz possess the power of human speech, the Wizard naturally addressed the birds as he would have spoken to human beings.)

But the birds made no reply. Instead, two of them stepped swiftly toward Dorothy and the Wizard, who had risen in surprise and were standing beside their chairs. The two birds flung themselves on the shadows cast by the girl and the man. Instantly the birds vanished, and Dorothy and the

Wizard found themselves staring in amazement at exact duplicates of themselves!

Sensing that he was confronted by some sort of evil magic, the Wizard made an effort to reach his black bag of magic tools which rested on a nearby table, but it was too late. Caught in the Mimic spell, the little man was powerless to move. Dorothy's plight was the same; she could not so much as lift her little finger.

All this had happened in much less time than I have taken to tell it, and it was so sudden and unexpected that our friends had not even had time to cry out.

Now the Mimic form of Dorothy, speaking in Dorothy's own voice, said to the two remaining birds, "Seize them, Ebo and Styg, and see that my commands are fulfilled!"

One black bird grasped the form of the helpless Wizard, the other that of Dorothy. Then, flapping their powerful wings, the two birds passed through the windows and soared aloft, bearing their captives high into the heavens.

Swiftly they left the Emerald City. In a few minutes it was no more than a lovely jewel set in the farmlands around it. The birds headed southeast in the direction of the Deadly Desert.

At times in their flight, when the captives were able to exchange glances, Dorothy read in the Wizard's kindly eyes a mute expression of concern for his little comrade. The girl tried to reassure him, but it was difficult to look brave when she was unable to move even an eyelash—and besides, Dorothy had to admit to herself, she didn't feel at all brave just now.

In another minute when Dorothy was gazing at the bird that was carrying her so swiftly through the air, she was startled to see the form of the creature shift and change. From a huge, eagle-like bird it changed to an enormous condor. Strange birds these were, Dorothy thought, which went about changing their shapes and stealing little girls and Wizards.

As they flew over the yellow land of the Winkies, the motion of the bird's body occasionally permitted Dorothy to look downward. Once she glimpsed, sparkling in the sunlight, the highly polished towers and minarets of a handsome tin castle. This, she knew, was the home of her old friend Nick Chopper the Tin Woodman, Emperor of the Winkies. Dorothy found herself wondering what the kind-hearted Nick Chopper would say if he could know that at this moment his dear friends were being carried high in the air over his castle, prisoners of two giant black birds! But there was no use speculating in this fashion. The Tin Woodman was powerless to aid them, even if he had known their plight.

Chapter Five

With a start Dorothy realized that the birds had crossed the border of Oz and were now flying over the Deadly Desert. The fact that they had left the Land of Oz behind them disturbed Dorothy greatly. Yet the little girl did not give way to fright. She had experienced so many strange and sometimes dangerous adventures in her lifetime, that she had wisely learned never to despair. The journey over the desert seemed endless. Despite the great height at which the birds flew, Dorothy was beginning to feel faint and ill from the evil fumes of the sands by the time they reached the border of the Land of the Phanfasms. However, once past the desert, she was revived by the fresh air.

Where were these great birds taking them? And why? As Dorothy pondered, she noted a sharp mountain peak jutting suddenly out of the gray, grim land of desolate waste and stone that lay below. Straight for the mountain flew the birds. In a few more minutes they descended with their victims to the entrance of the mountain. Passing through the stone portal, the Mimics retained their bird shapes, circling through the vast cavern of the hollow mountain. The cavern and corridors were deserted now that the sun was in the heavens, and the Mimics had returned to their underground caverns to rest after the night of revelry.

Styg and Ebo flew to a ledge of rock that jutted out from the mountain wall. Ebo muttered a magic word, and a crude stone door swung open, revealing a lightless cavern. Dorothy was thrust into the cave, and a moment later the Wizard was deposited beside her in the darkness.

Until now Dorothy had entertained a vague hope that in some way the Wizard's magic powers would come to their rescue. But since the little man had none of his magic tools with him, and could not speak to utter an incantation, nor move to make the motions of a charm, Dorothy realized that he was quite as powerless as she.

CHAPTER 6
Dorothy and the Wizard Speak Strangely

OOMPH!" puffed the Scarecrow.

"Whooosh!" gasped the Patchwork Girl.

Colliding suddenly as they met headlong at a sharp turn in the garden path, both the Scarecrow and the Patchwork Girl tumbled in a heap on the garden walk.

A moment later they had risen to sitting positions and were regarding each other comically.

The Patchwork Girl was a sorry sight. The high-grade cotton in her patchwork or "crazy quilt" body was bunched together in all the wrong places. After running and dancing a great deal that morning—as she always did—the Patchwork Girl's body had sagged and she had grown dumpy in appearance. When this happened she always lay down and rolled about until she had resumed her original plump shape. Now after her abrupt meeting with the Scarecrow her figure was in bad need of attention. The pointed toes of the red leather shoes sewn on her feet stood straight up. Her fingers, carefully formed and fitted with gold plates for finger nails, dug into the path on which she sat. Her shock of brown yarn hair hung down over her suspender button eyes and over her ears, which were made of thin plates of gold. Between the two rows of pearls sewn in her mouth for teeth, her scarlet plush tongue stuck out impudently at the Scarecrow.

The Patchwork Girl's brains were slightly mixed, containing among other qualities a dash of poesy, which accounted for her habit of breaking into rhymes and jingles when it was least expected. Now she was too surprised to speak. She had been brought to life in the first place by a magic powder, and since she was always jolly and good-natured, the Patchwork Girl was a prime favorite among the Oz folks. Nicknamed Scraps, the queer girl laughed at dignity and liked nothing better than to dance and sing. It was impossible to be downcast for long in the company of this merry, carefree creature.

"Why don't you look where you're going, Scraps?" said the Scarecrow ruefully, as he brushed his blue Munchkin farmer trousers.

"Now that you mention it," replied the Patchwork Girl reprovingly, "I don't have X-ray eyes, so

I couldn't see through to the other side of the hedge where I was going."

"All right," said the Scarecrow, as he rose to his feet. "Please accept my humble apologies." The straw man gallantly assisted the Patchwork Girl to stand. "There's no harm done. The spill was as much my fault as it was yours. I was thinking so deeply that I didn't see you."

"What were you thinking about?" asked Scraps.

"Dorothy," replied the Scarecrow with a sigh. "Tell me, Scraps, have you seen her today?"

"Not once," answered the Patchwork Girl, combing her yarn hair with her fingers.

"Until a few minutes ago, I've spent the entire day with Aunt Em who sewed tight some of my stitches that were coming loose, sewed on my eyes with new thread, so I wouldn't lose 'em, and sewed on a new pair of red shoes, as I'd worn holes in my old ones. Now I'm as good as new!"

"Well," replied the Scarecrow, with his broad smile, "that may be true, but I'd say no matter in how good condition you are, you're always just sew-sew."

The smile quickly faded from the straw man's painted face as he continued seriously, "Scraps, I'm worried about Dorothy."

"Don't worry about Dorothy; she's able to take care of herself," said practical Scraps.

"You don't understand," explained the Scarecrow. "You see, yesterday after Ozma and Glinda left for the Forest of Burzee, Dorothy asked me to help her plan a banquet to celebrate their return. Dorothy wanted me to think up some ideas for the entertainment to accompany the dinner. I agreed to set my famous brains to work on the problem and spent all last night in deep thought. This morning, bright and early, I rushed to Dorothy and started to tell her the ideas I had. You can imagine my surprise when Dorothy stared at me as though she hadn't the faintest idea what I was talking about, and then turned and walked away from me."

The Scarecrow paused, his brow wrinkled with perplexity. "I don't understand it," he continued. "It isn't like our sweet little Dorothy to be rude or absent-minded. She and the Wizard have been in Ozma's Chamber of Magic all day and I tried twice to see her, but each time she said she couldn't be disturbed."

"Come to think of it," replied Scraps quickly, "Aunt Em remarked that she couldn't understand why Dorothy hadn't been in to see her. Dorothy always visits her Aunt Em and Uncle Henry at least once a day. But maybe she's busy ruling while Ozma's away." This explanation failed to satisfy the Scarecrow.

He was gazing in the distance down the garden path. "Isn't that Trot and Cap'n Bill sitting on that bench over there?"

"Whoop ti doodle who?
Cap'n Bill and Trot
It is as like as not!"

sang the Patchwork Girl, turning a handspring and dancing toward the bench.

The Scarecrow followed, and he and Scraps were warmly greeted by little Trot and old Cap'n Bill. The Scarecrow repeated his story of the strange manner in which Dorothy had been acting, but neither Trot nor Cap'n Bill had seen Dorothy that day. The old sailor was silent for a moment, considering. Then he said:

"You know, it's funny; but I was tellin' Trot only a minute ago that the Wizard had me puzzled by the curious way he was behavin'."

"What do you mean?" asked the Scarecrow.

"Well," went on Cap'n Bill, "fer some time past I've been workin' on a boat fer Ozma an' her friends, so they could go sailin' on that lake jest outside the Emerald City. I had everythin' I needed 'cept fer some tools, so the Wizard lent me some o' his thet get the work done extra fast, 'cause they're magic tools. The boat's nearly finished—a handsome craft if I do say so myself. All she needs to make 'er trim is a coat o' paint. I thought it would be nice to have 'er finished as a sort of surprise fer Ozma when she returns from this here fairy conclave, so I asked the Wizard to lend me his magic paint bucket and brush—the bucket always stays full, no matter how much paint you use from it, an' the brush paints any color you want from the same bucket o' paint. Well, the Wizard jest gave me a funny sort o' look and walked away, mumblin' somethin' about bein' busy and havin' somethin' important to do. 'Tain't like the Wizard at all. Somethin' ailin' him," concluded Cap'n Bill, wagging his grizzled head.

"Then it's the same thing that's ailing Dorothy," remarked the Scarecrow sagely.

The four old friends were silent, each turning over the problem in his own mind.

The bench on which Trot and Cap'n Bill were sitting was in front of a high hedge—so high that none of them could see over it. On the other side of the thick hedge ran another garden path. Suddenly they heard footsteps, as if several people were hurrying down the garden path which was hidden from their view. While they listened, wondering who it could be, the footsteps halted just opposite them on the other side of the hedge. Before they could call out a greeting, they recognized the voice of the Wizard saying: "We can talk here. There's no one about. Now tell me; why are we wasting time in the garden?"

"Because," it was the voice of Dorothy replying, "it would look suspicious if we did not leave the Chamber of Magic occasionally."

"Have you found the spell yet?" asked the Wizard's voice.

"Not yet," replied Dorothy's voice. "I've been through only half of Ozma's magic record books. Give me time—it's there. And I'll find it!"

"Time!" replied the Wizard's voice, raised in excitement. "We have no time to lose! Do you realize that Ozma and Glinda will be back in a day and a half? We must find the spell before then if we don't want Ozma to wreck our plans and rob us of the chance we have waited for!"

"Never fear," asserted Dorothy's voice. "I'll find the spell long before Ozma and Glinda return. We'll be ready for those two when they do come back!"

Gradually the voices subsided, as the two walked slowly down the garden path toward the Royal Palace.

On the other side of the hedge, Trot, Cap'n Bill, Scraps and the Scarecrow stared at one another in bewilderment. What could this mean? It was incredible that Dorothy and the Wizard could be plotting against their dearest friends, Ozma and Glinda.

In the Cavern of the Doomed

Neither Dorothy nor the Wizard could tell how long they lay in their cavern prison deep in hollow Mount Illuso, but it is certain that minutes seemed like hours to them.

While the Wizard had recognized the country to which he and Dorothy had been carried as the Land of the Phanfasms, he was not aware of the existence of Mount Illuso and its Mimic dwellers. He was sure, however, that the creatures who had captured Dorothy and him were not Phanfasms. He had seen the Phanfasms when those evil creatures had once attempted to invade Oz, and they bore no resemblance to the beings who had made Dorothy and him captives.

Dorothy found some comfort in telling herself that as soon as Ozma and Glinda returned to the Emerald

In the Cavern of the Doomed

City the imposters would be detected and she and the Wizard speedily rescued. But what if Ozma and Glinda were deceived? How long would she and the Wizard be kept in the cave? What wicked plot was behind all this? And just how powerful and clever were the creatures who had captured her and the Wizard?

Suddenly something happened that banished all these puzzling questions. There was a light in the cavern! The two prisoners could see each other! True, the light was feeble, but it was increasing steadily in strength.

As the light grew more brilliant, Dorothy felt pleasantly warm and glowing, as though she were lying in the bright sunlight. And then to her intense joy the little girl realized that the spell cast on her was broken. The light had released her. She was free to move about as she pleased.

Chapter Seven

Dorothy jumped happily to her feet. The Wizard, too, was freed from the spell, and a moment later was standing, smiling broadly with satisfaction. "Was the light your magic, Wizard?" asked Dorothy eagerly.

"No, my dear, I had nothing to do with the light," replied the Wizard.

"But I wonder who or what turned it on?" said Dorothy. "Could it be a trick, do you think?" she asked after a moment's hesitation.

"No, I believe not," replied the Wizard. "There would be no point in our captors troubling themselves to enchant us and make us prisoners, and then release us from the enchantment. I believe we will find this light is a part of a greater mystery than we know anything about."

"Well, seems to me there's plenty of mystery about everything that's happened today," said Dorothy. "What are we going to do now, Wizard?"

"Explore our prison," answered the little man promptly.

Dorothy looked about her. They were entirely surrounded by the solid stone walls of the cavern, which was about one-hundred feet square. She could detect no sign of the door by which they had entered.

"Look, Wizard," Dorothy exclaimed. "See how the light shines from one small point in the far end of the cavern?"

"Yes," agreed the Wizard, "it's almost as if someone had built a powerful flashlight into the stone wall. Come, let's examine the light more closely."

In the Cavern of the Doomed

The two walked to the opposite side of the cavern and found that, as Dorothy had observed, the flood of light originated from one small point. This point was a circular bit of stone, round and polished, and no larger than a small button.

"Why," exclaimed Dorothy, "it looks 'zactly like the button of an electric light switch! Wonder what would happen if I pressed it?"

Impulsively Dorothy reached out and pressed the button of rock with her finger. In the deep silence that filled the cave, the two adventurers detected a far-away humming sound, like the whirring of wheels in motion. As Dorothy and the Wizard listened, the sound grew louder.

"What do you suppose it is?" whispered Dorothy.

"I haven't the faintest idea," said the Wizard, "but I don't think we'll have to wait long to find out."

At last the whirring noise seemed to be just opposite them on the other side of the stone wall. It stopped completely and there was silence. A second later a section of the stone wall swung outward, and Dorothy and the Wizard found themselves staring into a small room—much like the car of an elevator. The car was painted bright blue, trimmed with red and gold, and sitting on a small stool was a curious little man.

CHAPTER 8
Toto Makes a Discovery

"Where's Dorothy?" Toto asked pretty little Jellia Jamb, Ozma's maid, as he paused outside the door of Dorothy's apartment early in the morning of the day after Ozma and Glinda departed.

"She's gone up to the Wizard's rooms in the tower," replied Jellia Jamb.

"Thanks," said Toto. "I imagine Dorothy will have her hands full while Ozma is gone."

With this, the little dog trotted down the corridor, philosophically seeking some other amusement. He hadn't gone very far before he was hailed by Betsy Bobbin, who appeared with a small wicker basket on her arm.

Toto Makes a Discovery

"Hello, Toto!" Betsy called. "Want to go with Hank and me? I'm going to pick wild flowers in the green fields outside the Emerald City and Hank's coming along. I have a nice picnic lunch packed," the girl added, indicating the basket she carried.

Now there were few things Toto liked better than to get out in the country and frolic in the fields, so the little dog accepted the invitation gratefully.

A short time later Betsy, her devoted companion, Hank the Mule, and Toto arrived at the gates of the Emerald City and were greeted by Omby Amby, the Soldier with the Green Whiskers. He was very tall and wore a handsome green and gold uniform with a tall plumed hat. His long, green beard fell below his waist making him look even taller. In addition to being the Keeper of the Gates, Omby Amby was also the Royal Army of Oz, Princess Ozma's Body-Guard and the Police Force of the Emerald City. You might suppose that, holding all these offices, Omby Amby was a very busy man. To the contrary, so seldom was there ever any breaking of the Oz laws—which were all just and reasonable—that it had been many years since the Soldier with the Green Whiskers had acted in any of his official capacities other than that of Keeper of the Gates.

As Omby Amby unlocked the gates for them, Betsy promised to bring him a bouquet of flowers for his wife, Tollydiggle.

Outside the Emerald City lay pleasant, gently rolling fields in which buttercups and daisies grew in profusion. Sniffing the fresh country air, Toto ran happily across the field. Hank hee-hawed loudly and fell to munching the tall field grass. Betsy was delighted with the hundreds of pretty flowers and gathered several large bouquets.

Shortly after noon the happy trio sought the shade of a large tree. Nearby, a spring of cool, crystal-clear water bubbled from a mossy bank and flowed across the field as a tiny brook. Betsy opened her basket and took out sandwiches, hard boiled eggs, potato salad and other picnic delicacies, which she and Toto shared. Betsy offered Hank a peanut butter sandwich, but the Mule refused disdainfully, saying, "No, thank you, Betsy, I much prefer this fresh green grass."

"Well, don't eat too much of it," advised the girl, "or you'll get the colic."

The mule winked one eye at Toto and replied, "I'd be much more likely to get the colic if I ate your strange human foods."

After they had eaten and refreshed themselves with the water of the spring, they rested for a time in the cool shade of the tree, and then leisurely made their way back to the Emerald City. At the city's gates, Omby Amby welcomed them back and gratefully accepted the bouquet Betsy gave him for Tollydiggle.

Arriving at the palace, the three friends said good-bye, Betsy going to her apartment, while Hank made his way to the Royal Stables to talk with his cronies, the Cowardly Lion and the Hungry Tiger.

Jellia Jamb tripped down the palace steps on an errand, and Toto called to her, "Is Dorothy still busy?"

"Yes," answered Jellia Jamb, "she and the Wizard have been in Ozma's Chamber of Magic all afternoon."

This did not strike the little dog as strange. He knew Ozma might have left instructions for Dorothy and the Wizard to carry out in the Chamber of Magic.

As it was now nearly mid-afternoon, Toto decided to have a nap in the garden. Curling up in the cool earth under a large rose bush, he fell asleep, telling himself that he would awaken in time for dinner, when he would surely see Dorothy. Toto knew that however busy Dorothy and the Wizard might be, they would leave the Chamber of Magic and appear for dinner—always a festive occasion in the Grand Dining Room of the Royal Palace.

* * * *

Promptly at seven o'clock, the inhabitants of the Royal Palace began to gather in the Grand Dining Room. Cap'n Bill and Trot took their accustomed places at the table, as did Betsy Bobbin, Button Bright, the Shaggy Man, Aunt Em and Uncle Henry. While the Scarecrow, the Patchwork Girl and Tik-Tok the Machine Man were non-flesh and could not partake of the food, nevertheless they had their places at the table. For these dinners were as much occasions for the enjoyment of merry conversation, as they were for satisfying hunger and thirst.

At the far end of the room was a separate table, shared by the animal companions of the Oz people. At this table were set places with the proper foods for Hank the Mule, the Cowardly Lion, the Hungry Tiger, Billina the Yellow Hen, Eureka the Pink Kitten, the Woozy, Toto and the Sawhorse. Although the Sawhorse was made of wood and required no food and seldom took part in the conversation, nevertheless the odd steed enjoyed listening to the table talk of the others.

Everyone was at his place except Dorothy, the Wizard and Toto—and of course Ozma's chair at the head of the table was vacant. Dorothy's place was at Ozma's right, while the Wizard sat at her left. A few minutes later, King Umb and Queen Ra, having decided that it would arouse too much comment if they were absent from the dinner, entered the sumptuous dining room and took their places on either side of Ozma's vacant chair. Now only Toto remained absent.

The truth was that the little dog had overslept and had awakened from his nap to find the shadows lengthening across the garden. Realizing he was late for dinner, Toto hurried to the nearest palace entrance and ran as quickly as he could to the Grand Dining Room.

As he entered, the first course of the meal was being served, and a ripple of conversation rose from the two tables. The Scarecrow and Scraps were chatting together. Betsy was telling Trot about the lovely wild flowers she had found, and the Cowardly Lion and the Hungry Tiger were discussing a visit they planned to their old jungle home in the forest far to the south in the Quadling Country.

In spite of the apparent atmosphere of merriment, this gathering was not at all like the lively company that usually assembled in the dining room for the evening meal. First of all, the absence of the radiant Ozma was keenly felt by the entire gathering, and this automatically subdued the spirit of the occasion. Next, no one at the table had failed to note and wonder at the fact that Dorothy and the Wizard—usually so cheerful and cordial—had merely nodded unsmilingly to their assembled friends as they had taken their places at the head of the table. Finally, Scraps, the Scarecrow, Trot and Cap'n Bill, unable to forget the strange conversation they had overheard in the

Toto Makes a Discovery

garden earlier in the day, stole curious glances at Dorothy and the Wizard, seeking some clue to their unusual behavior.

As Toto trotted into the dining room, his bright little eyes immediately sought out his mistress. Toto stopped short; his body became tense with excitement. He barked loudly and then growled, "Where's Dorothy?"

In the silence that fell over the dining room at the dog's unusual actions, Toto repeated his question. "Where's Dorothy?" he demanded.

The Scarecrow was staring earnestly at Toto. "Why, here's Dorothy," the straw man answered. "Right here, where she always sits."

"You're wrong—all of you are wrong," growled Toto ominously. The little dog was quivering with excitement. "Whoever that is sitting there might fool the rest of you, but she can't deceive me. She's not Dorothy at all. Something's happened to Dorothy!"

CHAPTER 9
Mr. and Mrs. Hi-Lo

Step right in, folks! Watch your step, Miss. We're on our way up—next stop the top! Only two stops—bottom and top. Next stop's the top!"

The little man spoke with an air of importance, as he smiled at Dorothy and the Wizard from the stool on which he was perched in the car which the opening in the stone wall had revealed. They peered at him curiously.

"Shall we go in?" asked Dorothy, drawing a deep breath.

"To be sure," said the Wizard. "Anything is better than this stone prison."

"Ah, a philosopher, and a wise one, too," remarked the little man.

Mr. and Mrs. Hi-Lo

As soon as Dorothy and the Wizard were in the elevator—for such it proved to be—the stone door swung shut. At once the little man pressed one of several buttons on the side of the car and again they heard the whirring sound which had puzzled them in the cavern. Dorothy concluded it was caused by the machinery that operated the elevator. The little car was shooting upward with a speed that caused her ears to ring.

"Just swallow several times," advised the Wizard, sensing Dorothy's discomfort. "That will make equal the air pressure inside and outside your body. It's a trick I learned when I went up in my balloon to draw crowds to the circus back in Omaha."

Dorothy did as the Wizard suggested and found the ringing sensation disappeared.

"Who are you?" asked the Wizard gazing curiously at the little man. "And where are you taking us?"

"You don't know who I am?" exclaimed the little man with surprise. "After all, you know you did ring for the elevator, and since I am the elevator operator, naturally I answered. Allow me to introduce myself. My name is Hi-Lo and I am taking you to the only other place the elevator goes except for the bottom— and that's to the top of Mount Illuso. I assure you it's a far better place than the bottom!"

While he spoke, Dorothy had been regarding the little man who called himself Hi-Lo. He was very short, his head coming only to Dorothy's waist. He was dressed in a bright blue uniform with big, gold buttons. A red cap was perched at a jaunty angle on his head. His face was round and his cheeks as rosy as two apples. His blue eyes were very bright and friendly. But the oddest thing about him was that his clothes appeared to be a part of his body—as though they were painted on. And Dorothy concluded he was most certainly made of some substance other than flesh and blood.

"Ah, I see I've aroused your interest," remarked the little man with satisfaction. "Well, I'm proud to tell you that I am made of the finest white pine and painted with quick-drying four-hour enamel that flows easily from the brush and is guaranteed not to chip, crack, craze or peel. I'm easily washable, too; spots and stains wipe off in a jiffy with a damp cloth or sponge—no rubbing or scrubbing for me! And I suppose," Hi-Lo concluded vainly, "you've already admired my rich, glossy finish and beautiful rainbow colors."

Dorothy smiled at this speech, and the Wizard asked, "Tell me, Hi-Lo, do people live on the top of Mount Illuso?"

"Of course," Hi-Lo replied in his cheerful voice. "We have a thriving community of folks—Pineville it's called. But we're all very happy and contented," he went on hastily. "There's not a lonesome pine among us, although there are several trails on the mountain top."

"But are there no flesh and blood folks, like us?" queried the Wizard.

Before Hi-Lo could answer, the elevator came to an abrupt stop.

Mr. and Mrs. Hi-Lo

"Well, here we are!" announced Hi-Lo cheerily. He pressed another button. The door of the elevator swung open and Hi-Lo called, "All out! All out! Top floor— all kinds of wooden goods, the best pine to be had— pine tables, pine chairs, pine houses and pine people!"

Chapter Nine

Dorothy and the Wizard stepped from the elevator and surveyed the scene before them. Yes, this was certainly the top of Mount Illuso. The elevator exit was in a large stone wall, at least ten feet in height, that appeared to circle the edge of the mountain top. Before them spread a dense pine forest, while a small path led from the elevator to a tiny cottage that stood nearby. The cottage was painted bright blue with trim white shutters, and smoke was rising cheerily from its red brick chimney.

"Right this way! Just follow me, folks," said Hi-Lo, trotting along the path to the cottage, his little wooden legs moving with surprising speed. "Mrs. Hi-Lo will certainly be surprised to see you. You are a real event—the very first visitors we have ever had from down below."

As they approached the tiny cottage, the front door swung open, and a little woman stood in the doorway. She was even smaller than Hi-Lo, and like him was made of wood and painted with the same bright enamels. She wore a blue and white apron over a red polka-dot dress. On her head was a trim little lace cap.

"My goodness!" she beamed. "Visitors at last! Do come in and make yourselves comfortable."

The Wizard found it necessary to bend over to get in the doorway, so small was the cottage. Once inside, his head nearly touched the ceiling. The cottage was neatly and attractively furnished with comfortable pine chairs, tables and a large davenport drawn before a fireplace on which a log fire crackled cheerfully. The air was sharp on the mountain top, so the bright fire

was a welcome sight to the two wanderers. All the furniture glowed with the cheerful, gaudy hues of glossy enamel. Dorothy thought that the wholesome aroma of pine scent that filled the cottage was especially delightful.

"Great pine cones!" exclaimed Mrs. Hi-Lo. "You must be half starved. I'll get you something to eat in no time at all. Tell me, would you like a delicious cross cut of pine steak with pine-dust pudding, fresh, crisp pine-needle salad with turpentine dressing and a strawberry pine cone for dessert?"

Dorothy almost laughed aloud at this strange food, but the little Wizard answered courteously, "You are most kind, Madame, but I fear our systems would not be able to digest the delicacies you suggest. Perhaps you have something that meat folks like us could eat?"

"Of course!" cried Mrs. Hi-Lo. "How stupid of me! You are meat folks—too bad," she added critically. "It must be a terrible bother to take off and put on all those clothes and to keep your hair trimmed and your nails pared."

"Now, Mother, let's not draw unkind comparisons," cautioned Hi-Lo diplomatically, as he settled himself into a comfortable chair. "None of us is perfect, you know. Remember that spring when you sprouted a green twig on your right shoulder?"

"You are right," said Mrs. Hi-Lo with a laugh. "We all have our weak points." And with that the little lady bustled off into the kitchen.

Dorothy and the Wizard sat down gingerly on two of the largest chairs the room contained. But small as

the chairs were, they proved quite sturdy and readily supported their weight.

"Is there any way," asked the Wizard, "that we can leave this mountain top?"

Hi-Lo sat bolt upright in his chair and stared at the Wizard in amazement. "Leave the mountain top?" he repeated as if he couldn't believe his own ears. "Do I understand you to say that you want to leave this delightful place—this most favored spot in the universe?"

"We do," said the Wizard emphatically. "Our home is in the Land of Oz, and we desire to return there as quickly as possible."

"But why?" asked Hi-Lo. "No place could be as delightful as this mountain top. Just wait until you have become acquainted with it—our healthful, refreshing climate, our beautiful pine forest, our handsome village of Pineville and its delightful people! "

Mr. and Mrs. Hi-Lo

"Have you ever been anywhere else?" asked the Wizard quietly.

"No, never—but—"

"Then permit me to say," replied the Wizard, "that you are not qualified to judge. Little Dorothy and I have traveled in many strange lands all over the world, and we prefer the Land of Oz for our home."

"Well, everyone to his own taste, of course," muttered Hi-Lo, unconvinced and a trifle crestfallen.

Just then Mrs. Hi-Lo re-entered the room bearing a tray laden with steaming hot foods. At her invitation Dorothy and the Wizard pulled their chairs up to a table, and Mrs. Hi-Lo served the food on gleaming white enameled pine platters and dishes. There was savory vegetable soup, scrambled eggs, cheese, lettuce and tomato salad, chocolate layer cake and lemonade. The food was delicious and as Dorothy and the Wizard had not eaten since breakfast, and it was now nearly evening, they did full justice to the meal. Mr. and Mrs. Hi-Lo looked on with polite curiosity, marveling that the strangers could enjoy such odd food.

When they had finished, the Wizard sighed with satisfaction and sat back in his chair. "Where did you get this excellent food, if there are no human beings on the mountain top?" he asked.

"Oh, but there is one meat person like yourselves on Mount Illuso," said Mrs. Hi-Lo. "She is our ruler, and many years ago she gave me the magic recipe for the preparation of human food. As you are the first human visitors we have ever had, this is the first time I have had occasion to use the recipe."

"Who is this ruler of yours?" inquired Dorothy.

"She is a beautiful Fairy Princess, named Ozana," Hi-Lo replied.

"Ozana!" exclaimed Dorothy. "Wizard, did you hear that? Ozana—doesn't that sound an awful lot like an Oz name?"

"It certainly does," agreed the little man. "May we see this Princess Ozana of yours?" he asked Hi-Lo.

"I was about to mention," replied Hi-Lo, "that it was Ozana's orders when she appointed me Keeper of the Elevator that I was to instruct any passengers I might have to seek her out at her home in Pineville."

"Oh, let's go see her right away!" exclaimed Dorothy excitedly.

"Not tonight," objected Hi-Lo. "You would never find your way through the Pine Forest in the dark. You may stay with us tonight and be on your way to see Princess Ozana early in the morning."

Mr. and Mrs. Hi-Lo

Dorothy and the Wizard could offer no objection to this sensible and kindly offer of hospitality. Since it was now quite dark outside, and the little cottage was cheerful and cozy with the log fire casting dancing reflections in the brightly enameled furniture, they were quite content to spend the night there.

After several more questions about the ruler who called herself Ozana, Dorothy and the Wizard decided that Hi-Lo and his wife knew nothing more beyond the facts that Princess Ozana had created the pine folks and built the village for them to live in.

"Have you and Hi-Lo always lived here alone?" Dorothy asked Mrs. Hi-Lo.

The little woman's expression was sad as she answered, "No. Once we had a son. He was not a very good boy and was continually getting into mischief. He was the only one of our wooden folks who ever was discontented with life here on Mount Illuso. He wanted to travel and see the world. We could do nothing at all with him." Mrs. Hi-Lo sighed and continued, "One day a friendly stork paused in a long flight to rest on Mount Illuso, and the naughty boy persuaded the stork to carry him into the great outside world. From that time on we have never heard anything more of him. I often wonder what happened to our poor son," the little woman concluded in a sorrowful tone.

"How big was your boy?" asked the Wizard. "Was he just a little shaver?"

"Oh, no," replied Mrs. Hi-Lo. "He was almost fully grown—a young stripling, I should call him."

"And was his name Charlie?" inquired the Wizard thoughtfully.

"Yes! Yes, it was! Oh, tell me, Sir," implored Mrs. Hi-Lo, "do you, perchance, know my son?"

"Not personally," replied the Wizard. "But I can assure you, Madame, that you have nothing to worry about where your son Charlie is concerned. That friendly stork knew his business and left Charlie on the right doorstep."

The Wizard had a small radio in his apartment in the Royal Palace in the Emerald City, which he sometimes turned on and listened to with much curiosity. But he never listened for long, as he was subject to headaches when listening to anything but good music.

"Oh, thank you!" exclaimed Mrs. Hi-Lo. "It is such a relief to know that our Charlie turned out all right after all. There were times," the woman confessed, "when I had a horrible suspicion that he was made from a bad grade of pine—knotty pine, you know."

"There are those who share that opinion," murmured the Wizard. But Mrs. Hi-Lo was so overjoyed to hear of her son that she paid no attention to the Wizard's words.

Hi-Lo, who seemed totally uninterested in this conversation concerning his wayward son, merely muttered, "A bad one, that youngster," and then yawned somewhat pointedly and remarked that since their beds were far too small for their guests to occupy, he and his wife would retire to their bedrooms and Dorothy and the Wizard could pass the night in the living room.

Mrs. Hi-Lo supplied them with warm blankets and soft pillows, and then she and Hi-Lo bid them a happy good night. Dorothy made a snug bed on the davenport, while the Wizard curled up cozily before the fire. Just before Dorothy dropped off to sleep she asked, "Do you suppose this Princess Ozana has any connection with Oz, Wizard?"

"It is possible, and then again, the name may be merely a coincidence, my dear," the little man answered sleepily, "so don't build your hopes too high."

A moment later Dorothy's eyes closed and she was sound asleep, dreaming that Toto, in a bright blue uniform with big gold buttons and a little red cap, was operating the elevator and saying, "Right this way, Dorothy! Step lively, please. Going up—next stop, Princess Ozana!"

The Village of Pineville

Dorothy and the Wizard awakened bright and early the next morning, eager to pursue their adventures. Mrs. Hi-Lo prepared a hearty breakfast for them from her magic recipe and, as they made ready to leave the pretty little cottage, Hi-Lo advised them:

"Just follow the trail that leads through the Pine Forest and you will come to the Village of Pineville where Princess Ozana lives. You can't miss it, and if you walk steadily you should be there by noon."

Stepping from the cottage, Dorothy and the Wizard found the morning sun bright and warm and the air filled with the pungent aroma of pine from the forest.

"Good-bye!" called Mrs. Hi-Lo from the door of the cottage.

"Good-bye!" called Mr. Hi-Lo. "Don't forget to mention us to the Princess!"

"We won't," promised Dorothy. "We'll tell her how kind you've been to us."

In a short time the cottage was lost to their view, and the two travelers were deep in the cool shade of the Pine Forest. The trail over which they walked was carpeted with pine needles, making a soft and pleasant path for their feet.

Once when they paused to rest for a few moments a red squirrel frisked down a nearby tree and, sitting on a stump before Dorothy, asked saucily, "Where to, strangers?"

"We're on our way to see Princess Ozana," said Dorothy.

"Oh, are you indeed!" exclaimed the squirrel with a flirt of his whiskers. "Well, you are just halfway there. If you walk briskly you'll find yourselves out of the forest in another two hours."

"How do you know we are just halfway there?" asked Dorothy.

"Because I've measured the distance many times," replied the squirrel.

"I should think you would prefer to live nearer the village of Pineville," remarked Dorothy. "It must be very lonesome here in this deep pine forest."

"Oho! That shows how unobservant you mortals are!" exclaimed the red squirrel. "My family and I

wouldn't think of living anywhere but here, no matter how lonely it is. Know why?"

"No, I must say I don't," confessed the girl.

"Look at my tree—look at my tree!" chattered the

squirrel, flirting his big bushy tail in the direction of
the tree from which he had appeared.

"Of course!" chuckled the Wizard. "It's a hickory tree!"

"But I don't see—" began Dorothy in perplexity.

"What do squirrels like best of all, my dear?" asked
the Wizard, smiling with amusement.

"Oh, Wizard, why didn't I think of that? They like
nuts, of course!"

"Exactly!" snapped the little red squirrel. "And
since pine trees do not bear nuts and hickory trees
do—well, city life and fine company may be all right
for some folks, but I prefer to remain here in comfort
where I know my family will be well provided for."

And with that the wise little creature gave a leap and a bound and darted up the trunk of the one and only nut tree in all the Pine Forest.

Dorothy and the Wizard followed the pine-needle trail on through the Pine Forest until finally the trees thinned and they stepped out into an open meadow, bright with yellow buttercups. The sun was almost directly overhead by this time.

Below the two travelers, in a pretty green valley that formed the center of the mountain top, lay a small village of several hundred cottages, all similar to Hi-Lo's. The buildings were painted with glossy blue enamel and shone brilliantly in the sun. They were grouped in a circle about one large central cottage that differed from the others in that it was considerably larger, and, from where Dorothy and the Wizard stood, appeared to be surrounded by rather extensive gardens and grounds.

Dorothy and the Wizard followed the trail over the meadow to a point where it broadened into a street that led among the houses. The two travelers set out on this street, which was wide and pleasant and paved with blocks of white pine.

As Dorothy and the Wizard walked through the village, they saw that the cottages were occupied by wooden folks, much like Hi-Lo and his wife. A wooden woman was washing the windows of her cottage. A wooden man with wooden shears was trimming the hedge around his house. Another was repairing the white picket fence around his cottage. Tiny wooden children, almost doll-like they were so small, played in the yards. From one cottage a spotted wooden dog ran into the road and barked at the strangers.

"I suppose he's made of dog-wood," observed Dorothy with a smile.

Dorothy and the Wizard aroused much curiosity among the little wooden folk, most of whom paused in their work to stare at the strangers as they passed. But none of them seemed to fear the meat people.

A wooden lady approached them, walking down the street with quick, lively steps. On her arm was a market basket full of green pine cones. Pausing, the Wizard removed his hat and in his most polite manner addressed her.

"Pardon me, Madame. Can you tell me if this street leads to the palace of Princess Ozana?"

"Palace? What's that?" asked the woman with a puzzled expression on her face. "I don't know what a

palace is, Sir, but if you follow this street you will come to the cottage where our Princess Ozana dwells."

"Thank you, Madame," said the Wizard, and the little woman trotted busily down the street. In a few minutes more Dorothy and the Wizard had reached the central part of Pineville. Here a trim, white picket fence encircled a large area that seemed to be one huge flower garden with every sort of flower imaginable growing in it. In the exact center of this enclosure stood an attractive blue cottage, large enough to accommodate comfortably full-sized human beings. Just in front of the cottage was a pond of placid blue water. In the pond grew water lilies and all sorts of flowering plants that one finds in lakes and ponds.

The path that led from the entrance of the cottage divided at the pond's edge and encircled the water, meeting on the opposite side of the pond and running again as a single path to a gate in the fence before which Dorothy and the Wizard stood. Forming a bower over the gate was a white wooden trellis covered with roses. From the center of the pretty trellis hung a blue sign with these words in white enameled letters:

WELCOME

COTTAGE OF PRINCESS OZANA

WALK IN

"Well, I guess that means us," said the Wizard with a smile, as he read the sign and pushed open the gate.

CHAPTER 11
Princess Ozana

orothy exclaimed with delight as they stepped through the garden gate. She had no idea any garden could be so beautiful. Flowers of every known variety grew in profusion. Save for the mossy paths that wound through the garden, there was not a spot of ground that was without blossoming plants. As for the pond, it was like a small sea of lovely blossoming water plants. At the far edge of the pond Dorothy noted three graceful white swans, sleeping in the shade of a large flowering bush that grew at the edge of the pond and trailed its blossoms into the water. The air was sweet with the perfume of thousands and thousands of flowers.

"Oh, Wizard," gasped Dorothy, "did you ever see anything so lovely?"

"It is indeed a beautiful sight," replied the little man admiringly.

Here and there, throughout the garden, a score or more of little wooden men were busily at work. Some were watering plants from blue wooden pails, others were trimming blossoming bushes and hedges, some were digging out weeds, and others were building trellises for climbing vines. None of them took the slightest notice of Dorothy and the Wizard, so absorbed were they in their work.

Not far from where Dorothy and the Wizard stood, was a little maid, on her knees, digging with a trowel in the soft earth about a beautiful rambling rose bush that climbed above her on a blue trellis.

"Let's ask her where we can find Princess Ozana," suggested Dorothy.

A few steps brought them to the side of the maiden who wore a pretty blue apron with a pink petal design. On her hands were gardening gloves and her golden hair fell loosely down her back.

"I wonder," began the Wizard, "if you can tell us if the Princess Ozana is in?"

The little maid looked up, regarding the strangers with friendly curiosity. Dorothy saw that she was very lovely. Her eyes were as soft as shy woodland violets, and of the same purple hue; her skin as delicately colored as fragile petals, and her lips were like rosebuds.

"No," the maid replied with a suspicion of a smile. Dorothy glanced behind her and saw, scrambling from under a bush, a tiny kitten with pure white fur and china blue eyes. "Oh, what a darling!" she cried.

"This is Felina, my pet kitten," announced Ozana as she

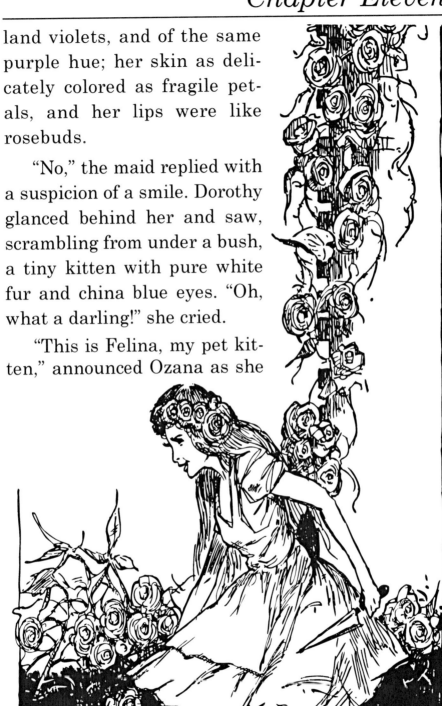

knelt and gathered the small bundle of fur into her arms. Ozana led her guests to the living room of the cottage, an attractive room, fragrant with pine scent and comfortably furnished with pine chairs, divans and tables.

Pressing a button set in the pine-paneled wall, Ozana bid her guests make themselves comfortable while she ordered lunch. A moment later a little wooden maid in a blue dress and spotless white pinafore, followed closely by a small wooden boy in a page's livery, appeared smiling in the doorway. The maid curtsied gracefully and the boy bobbed his head as Ozana said, "This is Dolly and Poppet, my maid and page. Dolly, will you and Poppet please prepare sandwiches and refreshments for us—my guests have traveled far and must be quite hungry."

"We are happy to serve your Highness," answered the wooden girl and boy in unison. With another curtsy and bow the maid and page disappeared from the room.

Ozana seated herself beside Dorothy and taking the little girl's hand in her own, while she smiled warmly at the Wizard, the Fairy Princess said, "Now, let us become acquainted."

"Well," began Dorothy, "this is the famous Wizard of Oz, and I am—"

"Princess Dorothy of Oz," Ozana finished for her.

"You know us?" asked Dorothy eagerly.

"To be sure, I know you," replied Ozana. "By my fairy arts I keep myself informed of all that goes on in the Emerald City. I recall when our Wizard first visited the Land of Oz in his balloon, and when the cyclone lifted your house into the air and carried you, Dorothy, all the way from Kansas to Oz."

"Why do you say 'our' Wizard?" asked the Wizard.

"Because I consider myself very close to the Land of Oz. I have a great fondness for all its inhabitants and especially for the Wizard who built the Emerald City and united the four countries of Oz," replied Ozana earnestly.

The Wizard blushed modestly. "As for building the Emerald City," he remarked, "I have said many times before that I only bossed the job—the Oz people themselves did all the work."

Dorothy nodded. "When I first heard your name, Ozana, I suspected it was connected in some way with Oz."

"I am called Ozana," stated the violet-eyed maid simply, "because I am a member of Queen Lurline's Fairy Band and first cousin of Princess Ozma of Oz."

"Wizard, did you hear that? Princess Ozana is Ozma's cousin!"

At this moment Dolly and Poppet reappeared bearing trays heaped with sandwiches and glasses of cool, fresh milk. Dorothy was so excited over the revelation Ozana had just made that she could scarcely eat.

While they enjoyed their food, Ozana and her guests exchanged stories. First Dorothy and the Wizard related their adventures. "I have no doubt at all," said Ozana, "that the two strange birds who took your forms were none other than King Umb and Queen Ra, the Mimic Monarchs."

"Did you say Mimics?" exclaimed Dorothy.

"Yes, my dear, Mount Illuso is the home of the dread Mimics."

"Oh," said Dorothy thoughtfully, "that explains a lot of things. Why, only the day before she left the Land of Oz, Ozma and I were discussing the Mimics."

The Wizard, who knew nothing of the Mimics, listened with interest as Ozana described the creatures.

"I don't understand," said the Wizard when Ozana had finished, "why you should be living alone on the top of this mountain in which such evil creatures as the Mimics dwell."

"That question is easily answered," replied Ozana. "Immediately after Queen Lurline enchanted the Mimics so that they could not attack the Oz inhabitants, she flew with me, her fairy companion, to the top of Mount Illuso. Here she left me, giving me certain fairy powers over the Mimics and instructing me that I was to remain here at all times as the Guardian of Oz to prevent the Mimics from doing any harm to the Oz people should the evil creatures ever succeed in lifting Queen Lurline's spell. I was not even permitted to leave the mountain to attend Queen Lurline's fairy councils in the Forest of Burzee."

"Then it must have been your fairy light that freed us from the Mimic enchantment in the cavern prison," surmised Dorothy.

"Yes, it was," Ozana admitted. "You see, after Queen Lurline departed from Mount Illuso and I was left alone, the first thing I did was to place the button of light in that cavern which the Mimics call their Cavern of the Doomed. I enchanted the light so that it would appear soon after prisoners were placed in the cave. I gave the light power to overcome the spell cast by the Mimics on their victims."

"Then you are responsible for the elevator and Hi-Lo, too," said the Wizard.

"Yes," replied Ozana. "I placed the elevator in the mountain and stationed Hi-Lo there to operate it. I did all this by my fairy arts. Of course the Mimics have no knowledge of my arrangements to bring about the release of their victims. I knew the escaped prisoners would find their way to me and I could aid them if I judged them worthy. But I never expected to find inhabitants of the Land of Oz in the Mimic Cavern of the Doomed!"

"How is it," asked the Wizard, "that the Mimics were able to capture Dorothy and me, despite the fact that we are inhabitants of the Land of Oz?"

"You must remember," said Ozana, "that both you and Dorothy came to Oz from the great outside world and neither of you was an inhabitant of Oz when Queen Lurline cast her spell over the Mimics. Hence you were not protected by that spell. It was for just such an unlooked-for development as this that the wise Queen Lurline left me on this mountain top."

"May I ask then," said the Wizard, "why you knew nothing of the flight of the Mimic King and Queen to the Emerald City?"

Ozana's face flushed slightly at this question, and she replied hesitatingly. "I must admit that I am fully responsible for all your troubles. But I plead with you to consider my side of the story. I have dwelt on this forsaken mountain-top with no human companions for more than two hundred years. At first I amused myself by creating the little wooden people and building their pine village for them. But it was too much like playing with dolls, and I soon tired. Then I busied myself with my garden, growing in it every variety of flower that exists. This occupied me for many long years.

"Please remember I had taken many precautions against the Mimics. I believed I could rely on my fairy light to free any prisoners in the Cavern of the Doomed, but apparently the Mimics took no captives they thought important enough to occupy the Cavern of the Doomed until they made you prisoners. And then my fairy light served me well. Can you find it in your hearts to forgive me that I did not spend all my time keeping guard over the Mimics through all those long years?"

"Of course. We understand, Ozana," said Dorothy, pressing the fairy maid's hand affectionately.

"And I must confess," continued Ozana with a grateful smile at Dorothy, "that had I not been so completely absorbed in my garden during the last few days, I would surely have known of Ozma and Glinda's departure from the Emerald City and your own plight."

The Wizard had been very thoughtful while Ozana was speaking. Now he asked, "Just what do you believe to be the plans of the two Mimics who are now masquerading as Dorothy and myself in the Emerald City?"

Ozana was grave at this question. "It is evident," she replied, "that King Umb and Queen Ra hope to take advantage of the absence of Ozma and Glinda to search for the counter-charm that would release the Mimics from Queen Lurline's enchantment and permit them to overrun Oz.

"Queen Ra must have discovered by her black arts that Queen Lurline had given the secret of the magical antidote into Ozma's keeping, knowing it would be safest with Ozma.

"It may be," added Ozana thoughtfully, "that if King Umb and Queen Ra have not discovered the spell by the time Ozma and Glinda return, they would even be so bold as to remain in the Emerald City, hoping they could deceive Ozma and Glinda as they have the rest of the Oz folks."

"What do you think they will do if they find the magic spell?" asked Dorothy fearfully.

The violet depths of Ozana's eyes darkened as she considered. "I don't like to think about that, my dear," she answered slowly.

After a moment's silence Princess Ozana brightened. "Come, now, let's not borrow trouble. The Mimic Monarchs have had so little time that I am sure they could not have succeeded in their search! We have nothing to fear now. However, I will spend the entire afternoon and evening in study, and by use of my fairy arts I will be able to discover just what King Umb and Queen Ra's plot is. With that knowledge we can act wisely and quickly to defeat the Mimic Monarchs."

"Do you think we should wait that long?" asked the Wizard.

"It is necessary," replied Ozana firmly. "I must have time to study Ra and Umb's actions during the past few days and to prepare myself to fight them. Remember, they are powerful enemies. Unless I am mistaken we shall be on our way to the Emerald City in the morning, and I shall be fully armed with whatever knowledge is necessary to defeat the Mimic Monarchs completely. Do not worry, my friends. I am confident I can bring about the downfall of King Umb and Queen Ra before Ozma and Glinda return to the Emerald City tomorrow."

"Of course you are right," assented the Wizard slowly.

"Now," said Ozana rising, "let me show you my garden of which I am quite proud. I am sure you will find it so interesting that you will regret you have only one short afternoon to spend in it. I have passed countless days in it and found it ever more fascinating."

The White Kitten, Felina, had finished lapping up the milk from the bowl placed on the floor for her by the little wooden maid. Dorothy knelt, cuddling the tiny creature in her arms.

"May I take Felina in the garden with us?" Dorothy asked.

"To be sure," replied Ozana. "I shall be far too occupied this afternoon to give her my attention."

As they stepped from Ozana's cottage into the garden, the Fairy Princess said, "I believe you will find my garden different from any you have ever seen. I call it my Story Blossom Garden."

CHAPTER 12
Story Blossom Garden

Now I will show you why I call my garden Story Blossom Garden," began Ozana as she advanced toward a rose tree laden with lovely blooms.

"You see, these are not ordinary flowers. They are fairy flowers that I created with my fairy arts. And the soil in which they grow is magic soil. Take this rose, for instance." Here Ozana cupped a large red rose in her hands. "Look into its petals, Dorothy, and tell me what you see."

"Why, the petals form a lovely girl's face!" Dorothy exclaimed in delight.

"And so it is with all the blossoms in my garden," said Ozana. "If you look closely into them, you will

111

see a human face. Now, Dorothy, put your ear close to the rose and listen."

Dorothy did as she was bid and quite clearly she heard a small but melodious voice say pleadingly, "Pick me, pick me, little girl, and I will tell you the sweetest story ever told—a love story."

Dorothy looked at the rose in awe. "What does it mean?" she asked Ozana.

"Simply that all the flowers in my garden are Story Blossom Flowers. Pick a blossom and hold it to your ear, and it will tell you its story. When the story is done, the blossom will fade and wither."

"Oh, but I shouldn't like any of the beautiful flowers to die," protested Dorothy, "even to hear their lovely stories."

"They do not die," replied Ozana. "As I said, these are no ordinary flowers. They do not grow from seeds or bulbs. Instead, as soon as a blossom has told its story it fades and withers. Then one of my gardeners plants it, and in a few days it blooms afresh with a new story to tell. The flowers are all eager to be picked so that they may tell their stories. Just as ordinary flowers give of their perfumes freely and graciously, so my flowers love to breathe forth the fragrance of their stories. A poet once said that perfumes are the souls of flowers. I have succeeded in distilling those perfumes into words."

"Can't the flowers tell their stories while they are still growing?" asked Dorothy.

"No," replied Ozana. "Only when they are separated from their plants can they tell their stories."

"Do all the roses tell the same love story?" Dorothy asked.

"No indeed," said Ozana. "While it is true that all the roses tell love stories—for the rose is the flower of love—all roses do not tell the same love story. Since no two rose blossoms are identical, no two blossoms tell the same story. It was my purpose in creating the garden to supply myself with a never-ending source of amusement as an escape from the boredom of living alone on this desolate mountain top. I was reminded of the Princess in the Arabian Nights tales. You will recall that she told her stories for a thousand-and-one nights. My story blossoms," Ozana concluded with a smile, "can tell many, many more than a thousand-and-one stories. There are many thousands of blossoms in my garden, and each blossom has a different story."

"You are certainly to be congratulated on your marvelous garden," said the Wizard. "It is a miraculous feat of magic," he added admiringly.

"Thank you," replied Ozana graciously. "And now I will leave you, as I must form our plans for tomorrow. I must ask you to excuse me from the evening meal. Dolly and Poppet will serve you, and when you are ready they will show you to your sleeping rooms. Good-bye, for the present, my friends."

Dorothy and the Wizard bid their lovely hostess good-bye and then turned to the wonderful garden of Story Blossoms.

Putting Felina on the ground to romp beside her, Dorothy dropped to her knees before a cluster of pansies. As she bent her ear over one of the little flower faces, it murmured, "Pick me, little girl, pick me! I'll tell you an old-fashioned story of once-upon-a-time about a wicked witch and a beautiful princess."

The Wizard found himself admiring the flaming beauty of a stately tiger-lily. Placing his ear close to the blossom, he listened and heard the flower say in a throaty voice, "Pick me, O Man, and hear a thrilling story of splendid silken beasts in their sultry jungle lairs."

Now Dorothy was listening to a purple thistle that spoke with a rich Scotch burr, "Pick me, little girrrl, an' ye'll make naw mistake, for I'll tell ye a tale of a Highland lassie for Auld Lang Syne."

Noticing a tawny blossom with vibrant purple spots, Dorothy placed her ear close to it. This was a harlequin flower and it said, "Pick me, child, and I'll tell you a wonder tale about Merryland and its Valley of Clowns, where dwell the happy, fun-loving clowns who delight in making children laugh." Dorothy remembered reading in a story book about Merryland and the Valley of Clowns.

Next was a Black-Eyed-Susan that murmured to Dorothy, "Pick me, and I will tell you the story of three things that men love best—black eyes and brown and blue. Men love them all, but oh, black eyes—men love and die for you!"

Dorothy smiled and moved on to a daisy which whispered to her in halting, doubtful tones, "Does he really love her? I shouldn't tell, but I know, I know—and I will tell if only you'll pick me, little girl."

"And I thought daisies didn't tell," Dorothy said to herself. She stopped before a rambling rose that spoke in a rapid, excited voice and wanted to relate a story of vagabond adventure in far-away places. Then a bright red tulip whispered about a tale of wind-mills and Holland canals and pretty Dutch girls.

At last the little girl came to a sunflower so tall that she had to stand on tip-toe to hear its words. "Pick me," the sunflower urged, "and hear my story of sun-baked prairies and western farm homes and great winds that sweep across the plains."

"I wonder," thought Dorothy, "if the sunflower would tell me a story about my old home in Kansas. There used to be a great many sunflowers on Uncle Henry's farm back there."

A tiny violet growing in a mossy bed caught the girl's eye, and as she knelt to hear its words, a shrill, unpleasant voice exclaimed, "Pick me! Pick me! Pick me immediately! I'll tell you a story that

will burn your ears off! All about Dick Superguy—
greatest detective in the world! He can't be killed—
he's all-powerful!" Dorothy was sure the shy little
violet hadn't uttered these words. While she looked
about to see where the rude voice was coming from,
one of the little wooden gardeners stepped up and
said apologetically, "Beg your pardon, Miss, it's just
a weed. They're always loud and noisy, and while
we don't care much for their stories, we feel they
have as much right to grow as any other plants.
Even a magic fairy garden has its weeds."

The Wizard had strolled over to the pond of placid
blue water, and placing his ear close to a green pad on
which nestled an exquisite water lily, he heard these
words, "Pick me, O Man, and I'll tell you a tale of a
magic white ship that sails the jeweled seas and of
the strange creatures that dwell in the blue depths."

Turning to a lotus blossom, the Wizard heard a
sleepy voice murmur, "Pick me, pick me. I'll carry you
afar to the secret islands of the never-ending nights,

where the winds are music in the palm trees and the hours are woven of delights."

Now that they had listened to the pleading voices of so many of the blossoms, Dorothy and the Wizard decided to pick some of them and hear their stories.

Dorothy's first selection was a Jack-in-the-Pulpit, which proved to be an unfortunate choice as the story the blossom told was preachy and sermon-like. She decided the blossom was a trifle green.

Next she tried a daffodil. The story this blossom whispered to her in silver tones was about a lovely Spring Maiden who went dancing around the earth, and at her approach all ugliness and coldness and bitterness vanished. In the Spring Maiden's wake appeared a trail of anemones and violets and daffodils and tulips, and gentle winds that caused new hopes to arise in the hearts of the winter-weary people.

The Wizard selected at pink carnation. This spicily-scented blossom told him an exciting story of intrigue and adventure in high places. It was a romantic, dashing story, full of cleverness and surprises.

Then the Wizard plucked a cluster of purple lilacs. Each of the tiny blossoms growing on the stem joined in a chorus to sing him a story of home and love, of patience and virtue and all the common things of life in which the poorest may find riches and happiness. Almost before Dorothy and the Wizard realized it, the shadows of evening were lengthening over the garden and Dolly and Poppet appeared to inform them the evening meal was awaiting them.

Dorothy picked up the White Kitten which had fallen asleep in the shadow of a nearby hedge, and she and the Wizard followed the maid and the page back to the cheery comfort of Ozana's cottage. They chatted happily over the good food served them by Dolly and Poppet. Felina had her bowl of milk on the floor, near Dorothy's chair.

Then, since they realized the next day was likely to be a busy and exciting one, they followed Dolly and Poppet to the rooms Ozana had prepared for them

and said good-night at their doors. The rooms were delightfully furnished with deep, soft beds and everything to make them comfortable for the night.

As Dorothy pulled the covers over her, and Felina snuggled into a small, furry ball at the girl's feet, Dolly reappeared with a poppy blossom in her hand.

"Here, Princess Dorothy," the thoughtful little maid said, "Listen to the story of the poppy blossom and you'll be sure to sleep well."

So Dorothy listened to the soft, slumbrous voice of the poppy and was asleep almost before the tale was finished.

What kind of a story did the sweet poppy tell? Why, a bedtime story, of course.

CHAPTER 13
The Three Swans

Dorothy was awakened by the sunlight streaming through the windows of her bedroom. Refreshed and eager for the adventures that lay ahead, she bathed and dressed and, with Felina in her arms, knocked on the door of the Wizard's room. The man was already awake and in excellent spirits as he greeted Dorothy. A moment later Dolly and Poppet came to lead them to the living room where Ozana was awaiting them for breakfast. The Fairy Princess, radiant with loveliness, was dressed in a simple, blue dress with a circlet of roses set in her golden hair. Dorothy thought this an excellent crown for the Princess of Story Blossom Garden.

The Three Swans

When the meal was finished, Ozana said, "It will please you to learn that my studies which I completed late last night revealed that the Mimic King and Queen have accomplished no real harm in the Emerald City. However, Queen Ra has succeeded in doing something that has surprised me. She has thrown up a magic screen about her activities which has made it impossible for me to discover whether she has found the spell that would release the Mimics from Queen Lurline's enchantment. It is logical to believe Ra has failed, since, if she had discovered the spell, she would surely have used it to permit the Mimic hordes to overrun Oz."

"But you cannot be sure. Is that it, Ma'am?" asked the Wizard.

"Yes, I am afraid so," Ozana admitted, frowning slightly.

"This magic screen that Queen Ra has devised baffles me and resists all my efforts to penetrate it. For this reason I think it would be wise for us to go as quickly as possible to the Emerald City. As you know, Ozma and Glinda will return from the Forest of Burzee this morning at ten o'clock. I would like to be present to greet them and to explain what has happened. There is no use causing them undue alarm. After all, I am responsible for the Mimics in regard to the Land of Oz," Ozana concluded thoughtfully.

"Well," said Dorothy, "I'm ready to go. How about you, Wizard?"

The little man's expression was grave as he answered. "The quicker we get back to Oz the better.

I have an uneasy feeling that we are not finished with the Mimics by any means."

"Then it is settled," announced Ozana. "Come, my friends, let us make all possible haste. We have no time to lose."

"May I take Felina to Oz with us?" asked Dorothy.

Ozana smiled. "Certainly, my dear. Only let us hurry."

Dorothy and the Wizard followed Ozana to the cottage door and down the path that led to the edge of the pond. The garden was fresh and lovely in the early morning. The side of the cottage that faced the morning sun was covered with blue morning glories. Dorothy regretted that there was no time for her to pick one of the delicate blossoms and listen to its story. Standing at the edge of the pond, Ozana uttered a soft, musical whistle. From under the low-hanging branches of a large bush that trailed into the water on the far shore of the pond, emerged the three graceful swans which Dorothy and the Wizard had admired the day before. The snow white birds moved swiftly across the water in answer to Ozana's summons.

"These are my swans which will carry us over the Deadly Desert to the Emerald City," said Ozana.

"They don't look big enough to carry even you or me, let alone the Wizard," said Dorothy doubtfully.

Ozana laughed. "Of course they are not large enough now, Dorothy, but soon they will be."

The three swans were now at the pond's edge, just at Ozana's feet. The Fairy Princess bent, touch-

ing the head of each of the birds gently with a slender wand which she drew from the folds of her blue dress. While Dorothy and the Wizard watched, the birds grew steadily before their wondering eyes. In a few seconds they were nearly five times the size of ordinary swans.

The Fairy Princess placed a dainty foot on the back of one of the swans, and then settled herself on the bird's downy back, motioning to Dorothy and the Wizard to do likewise. Dorothy stepped gingerly to the back of the swan nearest her. She found the great bird supported her easily. Holding Felina in her lap, the little girl nestled comfortably among the feathers. The Wizard had already mounted the third swan.

Seeing that the passengers were all aboard. Ozana signaled the swans, and with mighty strokes of their great wings the birds soared into the air. Dorothy looked behind her and saw Ozana's cottage growing smaller as the birds climbed higher and higher into the heavens. In a short time, they had left Mount Illuso so far in the distance that it was no longer visible.

The soft feathers of the bird that carried her, and the gentle motion with which it sped through the air, made Dorothy think of riding through the sky on a downy feather bed.

"Isn't it grand, Wizard!" Dorothy called.

"It certainly beats any traveling I ever did," admitted the Wizard. "It's even better than my balloon back in Omaha."

The Three Swans

Ozana's bird flew in advance, with the swans bearing Dorothy and the Wizard slightly to her rear on either side of her.

They crossed the border of the Land of the Phanfasms and soared high over the Deadly Desert. The swans flew even higher over the desert than had the Mimic birds. For this reason none of the travelers suffered from the poisonous fumes that rose from the shifting sands of the desert.

As they approached the yellow Land of the Winkies, Dorothy noticed that Ozana cast several anxious glances at the sun which was rising higher and higher in the heavens. It seemed to the little girl that the Fairy Princess was disturbed and anxious.

"Is anything wrong, Ozana?" called Dorothy.

"I cannot say for sure," replied Ozana. "Something has taken place in Oz of which I was not aware. I can feel the change now that we are actually over the Land of Oz. I am trying to discover what has happened by means of my fairy powers. I am afraid, too, that the journey is taking longer than I expected, and we shall not be able to arrive before Ozma and Glinda."

At a signal from their mistress the three swans quickened their already swift flight.

Again and again Ozana consulted the sun, and her appearance became more grave and worried as they approached the Emerald City.

Suddenly the Fairy Princess's expression changed. A look of anger and dismay clouded her face, and the next instant she cried out beseechingly:

"Forgive me, my friends! I now understand all that has happened. The Mimics have cunningly outwitted me!"

CHAPTER 14

The Mimic Monarchs
Lock Themselves In

Back in the Emerald City a great deal had been happening while Dorothy and the Wizard were adventuring on Mount Illuso.

You will recall that Toto had startled the Oz people by trotting into the Grand Dining Room and declaring that it was not Dorothy who sat at the head of the table. You see, in some ways animals are wiser than human beings. King Umb and Queen Ra were able to fool the Oz people just by looking like Dorothy and the Wizard, but they couldn't deceive the keen senses of the little dog so easily. Toto's animal instinct warned him that this was not his beloved mistress Dorothy nor his old friend the Wizard. When Toto made his astonishing assertion every eye in the dining room turned questioningly upon the Mimic King and Queen.

Suddenly Queen Ra leaped to her feet. Grasping King Umb by the arm and hissing, "Hurry, you fool!" she pulled the Mimic King after her and the two dashed from the dining room.

For a moment everyone was too startled to move—except Toto. He sped like an arrow after the fleeing monarchs.

The quick-witted Scarecrow broke the spell by leaping to his feet and following with awkward haste after the dog. Instantly there rose a clamor of startled exclamations and bewildered questions from the Oz people who were thrown into confusion by these strange happenings.

By the time the Scarecrow had reached the corridor, King Umb, Queen Ra and Toto were nowhere in sight. But the straw man could hear Toto's excited barking. Following in the direction of the sound, down one corridor and up another, the Scarecrow arrived in the wing of the palace usually occupied by Ozma, and found Toto barking before a closed door. The little dog's eyes flashed angrily.

Chapter Fourteen

When Toto saw the Scarecrow, he stopped barking and said, "I was just too late. They slammed the door in my face and now I suppose it is locked." The Scarecrow attempted to turn the knob with his stuffed hand and found that, as Toto suspected, the door was locked.

"Do you know what room this is?" Toto asked.

"Of course," replied the Scarecrow, "it's Ozma's Chamber of Magic."

"Yes," went on the little dog, "the same room where the imitation Dorothy and Wizard have shut themselves in all day. Why? I want to know! I tell you, Scarecrow, there's something awfully funny going on here."

The straw man was thoughtful. "I agree with you, Toto. Something is happening that we don't understand. We must find out what it is. I believe the wisest thing we can do is to return to the dining room and hold a council to talk this thing over. Maybe we will be able to find an explanation."

Silently the little dog agreed, and a short time later a group of the best-loved companions of Dorothy and the Wizard was gathered in a living room adjoining the Grand Dining room. The Scarecrow presided over the meeting.

"All we really know," he began, "is that Dorothy and the Wizard have been acting very strangely today—the second day of the absence of Ozma and Glinda. Toto insists that they are not Dorothy and the Wizard at all."

"Lan' sakes!" exclaimed Dorothy's Aunt Em, "I'll admit the child ain't been herself today, but it's downright silly to say that our Dorothy's someone else. I ought to know my own niece!"

"Em, you're a-gittin' all mixed up," cautioned Uncle Henry. "You jest now said Dorothy ain't been herself today—that means she must be somebody else."

"But who could look so much like Dorothy and the Wizard?" queried Betsy Bobbin with a frown.

"And why should anyone wish to deceive us?" asked tiny Trot.

Now Cap'n Bill spoke up. "S'posin'," began the old sailor gruffly, "that we admit fer the moment that this ain't the real Dorothy and the Wizard. Then the most important thing is—where are the real Dorothy and the Wizard?"

"That's the smartest thing that's been said yet," declared Toto earnestly, with an admiring glance at Cap'n Bill. "Here we are, wasting time in talk, when something dreadful may be happening to Dorothy and the Wizard. Let's get busy and find them quickly."

"Maybe they're lost," suggested Button Bright. "If that's the case there's nothing to worry about, 'cause I've been lost lots of times and I always got found again." But no one paid any attention to the boy.

With her yarn hair dangling before her eyes, the Patchwork Girl danced to the front of the gathering. "The trouble with you people," she asserted, "is that you don't know how to add two and two and get four."

"What do you mean by that, Scraps?" asked the Scarecrow.

"Just this," retorted the stuffed girl, saucily making a face at the Scarecrow. "What did we overhear Dorothy and the Wizard discussing today in the garden? Magic! They were talking about a magic spell which they hoped to find before Ozma and Glinda returned. All right. Now where did Dorothy and the Wizard spend most of the day and where have they fled just now to lock themselves in? To Ozma's Chamber of Magic!" The Patchwork Girl concluded triumphantly, "Mark my words there's magic behind all this, and the secret is hidden in Ozma's Chamber of Magic."

With his chin in his hand, the Scarecrow was regarding Scraps in silent admiration. "Sometimes," he said, "I almost believe your head is stuffed with the same quality of brains the Wizard put in mine."

"Nope!" denied Scraps emphatically. "It's not brains—just a little common sense." And with that the irrepressible creature leaped to the chandelier suspended from the ceiling and began chinning herself.

"Yes," agreed the Scarecrow with a sigh as he regarded her antics, "I guess I was wrong about your brains."

"But what are we going to do? That's what I want to know," demanded Toto impatiently.

"I believe," declared the Scarecrow finally, "there is only one thing we can do. We must go to Ozma's Chamber of Magic and try to persuade this strange Dorothy and the Wizard to admit us. If they refuse, then we shall be obliged to break open the door and demand an explanation of their mysterious behavior."

"Good!" exclaimed Toto. "Let us go at once."

They all filed out of the room and made their way to Ozma's Chamber of Magic. The door was still locked. Several times the Scarecrow called to Dorothy and the Wizard to open the door and admit them, but there was no response. Then Cap'n Bill stepped forward. He knew what was expected of him as the biggest and strongest of the group. He placed a shoulder against the door and pushed. The door creaked and yielded. Again Cap'n Bill pushed. This time the door yielded more noticeably. Upon the third trial the door suddenly gave way before the old sailor man's weight, and the Scarecrow followed by Scraps, Trot, Betsy Bobbin, Button Bright and the rest crowded into Ozma's Chamber of Magic.

CHAPTER 15

In the Chamber of Magic

When Queen Ra seized King Umb by the arm and fled with him from the dining room, the Mimic Queen was alarmed. She realized it was useless to attempt to deceive Toto, and she greatly feared the little dog would succeed in convincing the Scarecrow and the others that something had happened to Dorothy and the Wizard.

Fear lent speed to the Queen's feet as she ran down the corridor, dragging King Umb after her, with Toto in close pursuit. She slammed the door of the Chamber of Magic and locked it just in time to prevent Toto's entry. Then she flung herself in a chair, gasping for breath.

In the Chamber of Magic

When King Umb, who was even more frightened than his Queen, had got his breath and could speak, he said raspingly, "So this is the way your plan works—a miserable dog robs us of success!"

"Silence!" commanded Queen Ra angrily. "We are far from defeated. We still have time to find the magic spell. And we will! We were fools to give up the search and go to that silly dinner," she concluded bitterly.

She turned to Ozma's magic books and began feverishly leafing through them. For perhaps ten minutes she continued her search fruitlessly. Flung carelessly on the floor at her side was a great pile of books through which she had previously looked in vain for the magic spell. Only four books remained to be searched through.

While King Umb watched nervously, the Queen continued her frantic quest. Now only two books remained. The magic spell must be in one of these two volumes. Suddenly Queen Ra leaped to her feet with a cry of triumph. "I have found it!" she announced with exultation. She tore a page from the book and cast the volume to the floor. "Come," she urged, "Let us return to Mount Illuso as speedily as possible. Soon we will come again to Oz. But we will not be alone!" Both Ra and Umb laughed with wicked satisfaction.

Just then the Scarecrow called to Dorothy and the Wizard to open the door and admit them.

"Fools!" muttered Queen Ra. "In a short time you will all be my slaves."

Chapter Fifteen

Pausing to pick up Dorothy's Magic Belt, Queen Ra walked to a large French window that looked down on the palace courtyard. Turning to King Umb, she said, "These hateful shapes can serve us no longer, so let us discard them and be on our way." Instantly the figures of Dorothy and the Wizard vanished and in their places appeared two great, black birds with huge, powerful wings.

Just as Cap'n Bill burst open the door, and the Scarecrow and the rest crowded into the room, the birds flew from the window.

The little group hurried to the window and looked out. High above the palace and swiftly disappearing in the night, flew two enormous bat-like birds. The night was too dark and the birds too far away for any of the Oz people to see that one of the creatures clutched Dorothy's Magic Belt. While Queen Ra had not yet learned how to command the many wonderful

powers of the Magic Belt (or she would most certainly have used the belt to transport herself and Umb to the Mimic Land in the twinkling of an eye), nevertheless she had no intention of leaving the valuable talisman behind to be used by the Oz people.

More bewildered than ever, the Scarecrow and his companions turned from the window.

"I told you so!" declared Toto excitedly. "You see those creatures were not Dorothy and the Wizard at all."

"You are right," said the Scarecrow, "those great birds must be the same beings that we thought were Dorothy and the Wizard."

"Certainly," replied Toto. "You can see for yourself that Dorothy and the Wizard are not here."

It was true enough. There was no trace of Dorothy or the Wizard in the Chamber of Magic.

"But who were those creatures? And why did they want us to believe they were Dorothy and the Wizard? And what has happened to the real Dorothy and the Wizard?" the Scarecrow asked helplessly.

"Why not look in the Magic Picture and find out?" asked the Patchwork Girl, as she danced about the room.

"Of course, the very thing!" exclaimed the Scarecrow. "Why didn't I think of that myself?"

"Because your brains are of an extraordinary quality," retorted Scraps, "and you can't be expected to think common-sense thoughts."

The Magic Picture which hung on a wall in Ozma's boudoir was one of the rarest treasures in all Oz. Ordinarily the picture presented merely an attractive view of a pleasant countryside with rolling fields and a forest in the background. But when anyone stood in front of the picture and asked to see a certain person anywhere in the world—the painted picture faded and was replaced by the moving image of the person named and his or her surroundings at that exact time.

The Scarecrow and his companions gathered about the Magic Picture and the straw man said solemnly, "I want to see Dorothy and the Wizard." Instantly the painted scene faded and in its place appeared the interior of Hi-Lo's little cottage. Dorothy and the Wizard were just about to sit down to the food Mrs. Hi-Lo had prepared for them.

"I wonder who those two funny little people are?" murmured Trot, fascinated by the quaint appearance of Mr. and Mrs. Hi-Lo.

"They are not familiar to me," observed the Scarecrow reflectively, "nor have I ever seen a cottage quite like that one in the Land of Oz."

For a time the group watched in silence while Dorothy and the Wizard ate their food and conversed with Mr. and Mrs. Hi-Lo. But at length, as nothing of importance occurred, the Scarecrow said:

"Even though we don't know where Dorothy and the Wizard are, at least the Magic Picture has shown us they are safe for the moment and we don't need to worry about them."

"Why not use Dorothy's Magic Belt to wish Dorothy and the Wizard back here in the palace?" Trot asked suddenly as she stared at the images in the Magic Picture.

"An excellent suggestion!" agreed the Scarecrow, his face beaming. "Trot, I believe you have solved our problem," he said admiringly.

The Scarecrow knew that when Dorothy was not wearing her Magic Belt on a journey, it was always kept in Ozma's Chamber of Magic. So the straw man went there himself to get the belt. A few minutes later he returned and announced gloomily, "It's gone. The Magic Belt is nowhere in the Chamber of Magic. Either Ozma took it with her, or it has been stolen. The Magic Picture has shown us that Dorothy is not wearing the belt."

Disappointment was reflected on everyone's face, and for a moment no one spoke. Then the Scarecrow declared, "My friends, there remains only one more thing for us to do."

"What is that?" asked Cap'n Bill.

"One of us must leave immediately for Glinda's castle in the Quadling Country to consult Glinda's Great Book of Records. The book will provide us with a complete account of all that has happened to Dorothy and the Wizard."

"A wise suggestion," agreed Cap'n Bill. "Who will go?"

"I will," volunteered Dorothy's Uncle Henry quickly. "I want to do everything possible to bring Dorothy back

In the Chamber of Magic

to us and it 'pears to me we can't do much of anything until we know what has happened to her."

"Good!" exclaimed the Scarecrow. "You can leave at once. I will order Ozma's wooden Sawhorse to carry you to Glinda's Castle and back. But even though the Sawhorse is swift and tireless, you will not be able to make the journey, consult the Great Book of Records and return to the Emerald City before Ozma and Glinda come back day after tomorrow. That is too bad. The disappearance of Dorothy and the Wizard and all this mystery will not provide a very cheerful home-coming for Ozma and Glinda. But at least we shall have the information contained in the Great Book of Records, and then Ozma and Glinda will know best what to do."

Chapter Fifteen

Uncle Henry kissed Aunt Em good-bye and hurried to the Royal Stable where the Sawhorse was waiting for him.

"I understand," said the unusual steed, whose body and head were made from a tree trunk, "that we're going to Glinda's castle in the Quadling Country."

"That's right," nodded Uncle Henry. "And this is no pleasure trip, so go as fast as you can."

Glancing at Uncle Henry for a moment from one of his eyes which were knots in the wood, the Sawhorse turned, as soon as Uncle Henry was mounted, and dashed down the stable driveway into the street leading to the gates of the Emerald City. Once outside the city, the Sawhorse ran so swiftly that its legs, which were merely sticks of wood which Ozma had caused to be shod with gold, fairly twinkled. It sped with a rolling, cradle-like motion over fields and hills, and Uncle Henry had to hold on for dear life.

Perhaps I should explain that Glinda's Great Book of Records is a marvelous book in which everything that happens, from the slightest detail to the most important event taking place anywhere in the world, is recorded the same instant that it happens. No occurrence is too trivial to appear in the book. If a naughty child stamps its foot in anger, or if a powerful ruler plunges his country into war, both events are noted in the book, as of equal importance.

The huge book lies open on a great table, occupying the center of Glinda's study and is bound to the

table by large chains of gold. Next to Ozma's Magic Picture, Glinda's Great Book of Records is the most valuable treasure in Oz. The Scarecrow knew that by consulting this wonderful book, Uncle Henry would be able to discover exactly what had happened to Dorothy and the Wizard.

The Scarecrow and Scraps, having no need for sleep, sat before the Magic Picture all night long conversing quietly and occasionally glancing at the images of Dorothy and the Wizard as the picture showed them sleeping in Hi-Lo's cottage.

The rest of the Oz people retired to their bedrooms, but none of them slept well that night. They were far too worried over the plight of Dorothy and the Wizard to rest easily.

CHAPTER 16
A Web Is Woven

rriving at Mount Illuso early the following morning, King Umb and Queen Ra passed the day secluded in the secret cavern where the Queen was accustomed to study the dark sorcery of the Erbs and practice her evil magic. This cavern was so well hidden, far in the depths of Mount Illuso, and its location was so closely guarded, that only a few of the most faithful subjects of the Mimic King and Queen were aware of its existence.

While Queen Ra's shape was that of a woman, her body was covered with a heavy fur of a reddish-brown color, and her head was that of a fox with a long snout and sharply pointed ears. Two green eyes blazed with a fierce light from her furry face. In her hand the fox-woman held a brass whistle on which she blew a shrill blast. In answer to this summons came the Mimic known as Ebo. Ebo wore the body of a jackal with the head of a serpent.

"Go to the Cave of the Doomed and bring the two prisoners to me at once," the Queen commanded.

"Yes, your Highness," hissed Ebo as he swayed his serpent head in obeisance and left the cavern.

"We might as well have a little fun while we wait for midnight," grinned the fox head of the woman evilly.

King Umb appeared as a great, gray ape with cloven hoofs and the head of a man. From the center of his forehead projected a single horn. The man-face was covered with a shaggy, black beard which fell to the hairy chest of the ape-body.

"What do you intend to do with the girl and the man?" asked the gray ape.

Chapter Sixteen

"I shall practice transformations on the man, giving him a number of unusual shapes and then perhaps combine them all into one interesting creature. It is amazingly easy to change the shapes of humans, so it will not be much of a feat of magic. Then, just before we leave for the Emerald City, I shall change him into a salamander—a green salamander instead of the ordinary red kind, of course, since he is from the Emerald City—and then when we are over the Deadly Desert I shall drop him into the sands. Salamanders are the only creatures that can exist in the desert, so it will really be a merciful fate, since it will not stop him from living."

"And the girl?" prompted King Umb.

"I think I shall keep the girl chained in my cavern to amuse me when the excitement of conquering and devastating Oz is over and I am in need of diversion," said Queen Ra. While the Queen was relating her wicked plans, Ebo made his way to the Cave of the Doomed and was amazed and terrified to find it empty. How could there be an escape from the cave from which there was no exit save the single stone door which was always closely guarded? The jackal body of Ebo trembled with fear of the punishment he knew Queen Ra would be quick to inflict on him. But there was nothing else for him to do but to report the mysterious disappearance of the prisoners to the Mimic King and Queen.

Queen Ra received the news with a scream of rage. Blowing on her brass whistle, she summoned two other Mimics. Pointing to Ebo who cringed with fear, she cried, "Carry him away and cast him into the Pit of Forked Flames."

King Umb was uneasy. "I don't like this," he said. "How do we know that the two mortals will not interfere with our plans to conquer Oz?"

"Bah! What can two weak mortals do in the face of our might?" demanded the Queen derisively.

Knowing his wife's temper, King Umb refrained from reminding Ra that the mortals had somehow miraculously succeeded in escaping from the Cave of the Doomed. Instead, he merely shrugged his ape shoulders and said, "Just the same, I wish we were on our way to Oz now, instead of waiting until midnight."

Queen Ra glared at her husband. "I have told you that Lurline's enchantment can be broken only at midnight. Tonight at twelve, I will cast the spell which Lurline foolishly left in Ozma's possession. Since it is the antidote to the enchantment which protects Oz from the Mimics, Lurline knew Ozma would guard it most carefully. But we succeeded in stealing it. Once the spell is cast, the Mimics will be free in all their power to attack Oz and enslave its people. I tell you, Umb, the famous Land of Oz is doomed. In a few short hours it will be a shambles. Nothing can save it!"

* * * *

A few minutes before the hour of midnight, the Mimic hordes assembled in the vast domed cavern which forms that portion of hollow Mount Illuso that towers above the earth.

In the center of the cavern on a stone dais stood King Umb and Queen Ra. The Mimic Queen lifted her arms and immediately silence fell over the shifting mass of evil beings.

The Queen held in her hand a small box of black enameled wood. Placing the box on the stone dais before her, she raised the lid and muttered an incantation. Immediately there crawled from the box a scarlet spider as large as the Queen's hand. At the first word of the incantation the spider began to grow. In a few seconds its body was four feet in thickness, and its hairy legs sprawled to a distance of fifteen feet from its body which was covered with a crimson fur.

"Now go," Queen Ra commanded the spider, "and weave the web that will enmesh the fairy enchantment that hangs over us!" The Mimic hordes parted to make a path through their midst for the spider. The loathsome creature scuttled first to the wall of the

cavern, and then climbed up the side of the wall. In a few seconds it had reached the top of the cavern.

Then, moving with incredible speed, it wove a monster spider web of crimson strands as thick and tough as heavy rope cables.

Queen Ra watched silently until the fashioning of the scarlet Web was completed. At that moment she cried aloud for all to hear:

"So long as this web remains unbroken, the Mimics are freed from the enchantment cast on them by Lurline! The web is a snare and a net for Lurline's fairy enchantment and holds every remnant of it caught fast in its coils."

The Queen spoke triumphantly, and well she might, for the magic spell she had stolen from Ozma had worked perfectly.

"Come!" shouted Queen Ra. "Let us tarry no longer. We have waited too many years for this hour!"

With this the Mimic King and Queen assumed the shapes of giant birds and soared through the cavern to the stone portal. The throngs of their Mimic subjects followed, beating the air with great, leathery wings as they passed from the cavern into the night.

Soon the sky above Mount Illuso was darkened with the great numbers of the Mimic horde, and the light of the moon was blotted from the earth by the flapping wings.

Following the lead of King Umb and Queen Ra, they headed straight for the Deadly Desert and the Land of Oz.

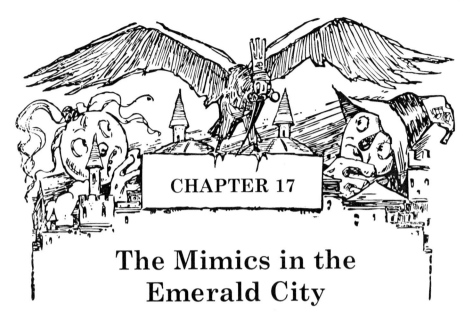

The Mimics in the Emerald City

On the morning when the Mimic hordes swept over the border of the Deadly Desert and the Winkie Country and on to the Emerald City, Button Bright and the Patchwork Girl were playing leapfrog in the garden of the Royal Palace.

Cap'n Bill was sitting nearby on a bench in the sun, carving on a block of wood with his big jack-knife. The old sailor man worked slowly and painstakingly, but when he finished he knew he would have a good likeness of Princess Ozma's lovely features carved in the wood. This he planned to mount as a figurehead on the prow of the boat he was building as a surprise for Ozma. Suddenly Button Bright, who had tumbled flat on his back, cried out:

"Look! Look at those birds!"

Scraps swept her yarn hair out of her button eyes and tilted her head back. The sky was darkening with

a great cloud of birds. And what beautiful creatures those birds were!

> "Birds of a feather
> Flock together.
> Red, blue, green and gold
> Match my patches, bold.

> "Not a gray topknot
> In the whole lot!
> See the popinjay
> Flirt its colors gay . . ."

cried the Patchwork Girl, dancing about in wild excitement.

"Stop it, Scraps!" commanded Button Bright who was nearly as excited as the stuffed girl.

"Trot, Betsy, Ojo, Scarecrow!" the boy called. "Come out and see the pretty birds!"

Of course this taking the forms of gorgeous plumed birds was a clever part of Queen Ra's cunning scheme. She knew the beauty of the birds, instead of alarming the Oz people, would fascinate them. The Queen hoped by this wily stratagem to take the Oz inhabitants completely by surprise with no thought of danger in their minds.

The scheme worked even better than Queen Ra dared dream.

Ojo the Lucky, Aunt Em, the Scarecrow, Betsy Bobbin, Trot, Jellia Jamb, and all the others came hurrying from the Royal Palace, while from the Royal Stable came the Cowardly Lion, the Hungry Tiger, Hank the Mule, the Woozy and others of the animal friends of the palace residents. Gathering in the gardens and courtyard, they all stared up in wonder at the beautiful birds.

Outside the grounds of the Royal Palace, much the same thing was happening throughout the Emerald City. Those people who were out of doors witnessing the spectacle called to those who were indoors, urging them to hurry out and see the lovely visitors. It was no time at all until every building in the city was emptied of its curious inhabitants.

This was just what the Mimics wanted. With the people of the Emerald City standing in the daylight, plainly casting their shadows, Queen Ra gave a signal and the Mimic birds ceased their slow circling in the sky for the enjoyment of the Oz people and dropped down to the city. King Umb and Queen Ra led those birds which settled in the palace courtyard and gardens.

A bird with brilliant scarlet and royal purple feathers and a topknot of gleaming gold alighted close to Trot. The little girl stepped forward with delight to stroke the bird's lovely plumage. Instantly the creature vanished and in its place stood a perfect duplicate of Trot, while the real Trot was frozen in her tracks, unable to move. Mystified at suddenly seeing two Trots before him, Cap'n Bill rose from his bench and started toward them. But he was confronted by one of the giant birds and an instant later the old sailor man was unable to move. He could only stare with amazement at an exact double of himself—wooden leg and all. Button Bright was about to leap playfully

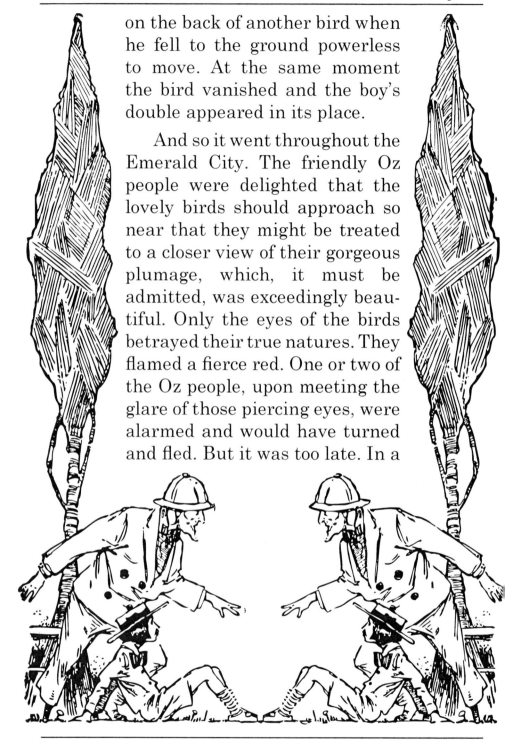

on the back of another bird when he fell to the ground powerless to move. At the same moment the bird vanished and the boy's double appeared in its place.

And so it went throughout the Emerald City. The friendly Oz people were delighted that the lovely birds should approach so near that they might be treated to a closer view of their gorgeous plumage, which, it must be admitted, was exceedingly beautiful. Only the eyes of the birds betrayed their true natures. They flamed a fierce red. One or two of the Oz people, upon meeting the glare of those piercing eyes, were alarmed and would have turned and fled. But it was too late. In a few minutes, all the human inhabitants of the Emerald City were made captives. However, the Mimics were able to steal the shapes only of human beings.

The Scarecrow, the Patchwork Girl, Tik-Tok, the Glass Cat, Billina the Yellow Hen, the Woozy, Toto, Hank the Mule, the Cowardly Lion and the Hungry Tiger remained unchanged. Fearing the mule, the lion and the tiger might prove dangerous because of their size, Queen Ra quickly placed a magic spell on the three beasts that caused them to fall on the courtyard lawn in a deep sleep.

The Scarecrow, Scraps, Tik-Tok and the others who had escaped the magic of the Mimics were completely confused by these sudden and baffling events. The stuffed girl rubbed her suspender button eyes and gazed with disbelief at two Button Brights—which one was it she had been playing with only a few minutes before? And there were two Aunt Ems and two Jellia Jambs! Wondering if the world had somehow suddenly become double, the bewildered Patchwork Girl looked about for her own twin.

Of all the horde of beautiful birds that had settled on the Emerald City, only two remained in the Royal Gardens. These were King Umb and Queen Ra. At this point the Mimic King and Queen cast off their bird forms. A strange man and woman suddenly appeared in the midst of the Oz people and the Mimic-Oz-people. The woman was big, raw-boned and red-skinned. Her hair was twisted on her head in a hard black knot, on which was set a small golden crown. The Scarecrow started with surprise when he

The Mimics in the Emerald City

saw that the strange woman was wearing Dorothy's Magic Belt. (Until now the belt had been concealed by the plumage of Ra's bird form.) Queen Ra had brought the Magic Belt with her because of its wonderful powers which she had been studying and which she felt would be useful in carrying out the conquest of Oz. Beside the woman stood a giant man with a flowing black beard and tangled black hair. His eyes were fierce and hawk-like.

Quickly Queen Ra uttered a command, at which a number of the Mimic-Oz-people leaped forward and proceeded to bind the non-human Ozites with strong ropes, which the magic of Queen Ra placed in their hands.

To his amazement, the Scarecrow found himself being made captive by Cap'n Bill and Ojo the Lucky. The straw man was wise enough to know that these twin likenesses were not really his old friends, Cap'n Bill and Ojo, so he resisted with all his might. But the poor Scarecrow's body was so light that the Mimics had no difficulty in fastening the ropes about him and pinning his arms to his sides.

Scraps was more of a problem. It required the combined efforts of the Mimic Jellia Jamb, Aunt Em, Betsy Bobbin and Button Bright to bind her. But even with these odds none of the Mimics escaped without scratches on his face from Scraps' gold-plated fingernails.

Tik-Tok, the Woozy, the Glass Cat and the rest were all securely bound in a few more seconds.

While our friends were being made prisoners, King Umb and Queen Ra hastened away to the Throne Room of the Royal Palace. There the prisoners of the Mimics were carried into the presence of the Mimic King and Queen. The Scarecrow and the others were shocked and outraged at the spectacle of the harsh-looking woman brazenly occupying Ozma's throne, while at her side stood the fierce-visaged man.

The Mimic Ojo and Button Bright lined up the captives before the throne, while Queen Ra regarded them scornfully.

"A pair of stuffed dummies, an animated washing machine, and a menagerie," she commented derisively.

"I demand," shouted the Scarecrow boldly, "that you release us immediately!"

"Ah! The famous Scarecrow of Oz!" gloatingly exclaimed Queen Ra. "And as brave as ever! I believe I will have your body destroyed by fire, first removing your head so that you will be able to entertain me with your wise thoughts. It would be a

shame," she added with sarcasm, "if such great brains were lost to the world."

Now the one thing in the world the Scarecrow feared was a lighted match, so it is no wonder that, brave as he was, he shrank before so terrible a fate as that proposed by the wicked Queen.

"You will not get a-way with this," warned Tik-Tok in his mechanical voice. "You will sure-ly be punish-ed for your wick-ed-ness and e-vil do-ing."

"And you are Tik-Tok the Machine Man," said Queen Ra. "As useless a pile of rubbish as was ever assembled. I shall have you carefully taken apart, piece by piece, and amuse myself in my spare time by trying to put you back together again like a jig-saw puzzle."

Chapter Seventeen

"My ma-chin-er-y does not per-mit me to fear," replied Tik-Tok calmly, "e-ven when I am thor-ough-ly wound up, so you are wast-ing your threats on me."

The evil Queen went down the line of captives, plotting terrible fates for each of them. Billina, she predicted, would soon be roasted for dinner. The Patchwork Girl would become a combination pin-cushion and personal slave. The Glass Cat would be melted down into marbles. Finally she came to the last of the prisoners—the square shaped Woozy—whom Ra promised to have chopped into cubes for building blocks.

It was at this moment that the Scarecrow became aware that with the exceptions of Hank the Mule and the Cowardly Lion and the Hungry Tiger, who lay sleeping in the courtyard, the animals of the Royal Palace were present—save the Sawhorse, who was at that moment swiftly bearing Uncle Henry back to the Emerald City from Glinda's Castle in the Quadling Country—and one other.

That other was—Toto!

CHAPTER 18

The Return of Ozma and Glinda

After his first sense of joy at finding that Toto had somehow escaped capture, the Scarecrow reflected more soberly that even though the little dog was free there was nothing he could do to rescue his friends from their desperate plight.

But the Scarecrow had been in dangerous situations before, so he did not give up hope by any means, while Queen Ra was gloating over her prisoners, the Scarecrow's famous brains were hard at work. Suddenly it occurred to the straw man that Ozma and Glinda were to return to the Emerald City at ten o'clock this morning. It was almost that time now. If only he could engage the wicked Queen in conversation until Ozma and Glinda appeared, then the Royal Ruler and the Good Sorceress might take their enemies by surprise. The Scarecrow was confident that Ozma would be able to deal with these usurpers to her throne.

With this plan in mind, the Scarecrow cried out in a bold voice: "I demand to know what you have done with Dorothy and the Wizard!" When he had witnessed the peculiar manner in which the gaudily plumed birds had assumed the shapes of his human friends in the garden, the Scarecrow had first suspected that these creatures were responsible for the disappearance of Dorothy and the Wizard. Then the sight of Dorothy's Magic Belt about the waist of the big woman had convinced him of the truth of his suspicions.

Queen Ra answered the Scarecrow with a scornful laugh. "You are quite brave, my blustering, straw-stuffed dummy, but your braveness will do you no good. As for your Princess Dorothy and the man who calls himself a wizard, you will never see them again. Furthermore," the Queen went on, "as soon as I have suitably disposed of you and the rest of these animated creatures and beasts, I will use the Magic Belt to transport the helpless bodies of all the Oz people in the Emerald City to Mount Illuso, where they will share the same fate as your Dorothy and her Wizard friend."

In spite of the assurance with which she spoke, the evil Queen was uneasy when she recalled the disappearance of Dorothy and the Wizard from the Cave of the Doomed. Had she underestimated the

Wizard's powers of magic? Queen Ra shrugged this thought from her mind. What had she to fear from two mere mortals? What had she to fear from anyone now? The Emerald City was hers and Oz was as good as conquered!

"Do not heed the threats of this wicked woman!" the Scarecrow called to his captive companions. "She is boasting too soon!"

At these words Queen Ra turned angrily upon the Scarecrow.

"Enough of your insolence, miserable wretch!" she cried. "I will show you who is boasting. Since you dare challenge me, I will destroy you immediately!"

Her eyes flashing with rage, Queen Ra leaped from the throne and moved toward the Scarecrow. When she was about six feet from him, Ra paused and muttered an incantation. Instantly dancing flames of fire leaped from the marble floor of the throne room, making a circle around the Scarecrow. With a smile of satisfaction, Queen Ra resumed her place on Ozma's throne to enjoy the spectacle in comfort.

The dancing circle of fire moved swiftly inward. As the blazing circle grew smaller in circumference, the flames leaped ever higher and closer to the helpless Scarecrow, who stood in the circle's exact center. The leaping fire had moved so close to the Scarecrow that it almost scorched his stuffed clothing. The friends of the Scarecrow watched in horror. Prisoners themselves, there was nothing they could do to save their old comrade from this terrible fate.

WHISH!

There was a sudden rush of air, and in the center of the throne room stood Princess Ozma and Glinda the Good on the exact spot from which they had vanished three days before.

Ozma swept the throne room with a glance that instantly comprehended the Scarecrow's great danger. In another moment her old friend would be reduced to a pile of smoldering ashes. Quick as a flash, the little Princess pointed her fairy wand at the flames that were licking the straw man's boots. While the onlookers blinked, the flames vanished. A long sigh of relief went up from the Scarecrow's friends.

Queen Ra was glaring with terrible rage at the Royal Ozma, who advanced calmly toward the

wicked Queen with an expression of stern dignity on her girlish features.

"Who are you, and what are you doing on my throne?" Ozma asked.

"Your throne no longer!" replied Ra harshly. "For you are no longer ruler of the Land of Oz. Instead you are my prisoner, and soon I will make it impossible for you to interfere with my plans as you have just done."

The stately Glinda spoke now, her voice grave and thoughtful.

"I believe I know who you are," she said. "You must be the Queen of the evil Mimics. I have read about you in my Great Book of Records."

"If this is true," said Ozma sorrowfully, "then your Mimic hordes are these creatures who so closely resemble my own beloved subjects, while the true Oz people are robbed of the power of motion by your evil spell."

"Good!" sneered Ra. "I am glad you understand everything so well. You have not a friend in the Emerald City to aid you. Every one of your subjects in the city is a victim of the Mimic magic. Soon this will be true of all the Land of Oz. I am sure you will agree with me," Queen Ra went on mockingly, "that it is only fair and just that you should share your subjects' fate. Indeed I know you are so foolishly loyal that you would not escape and leave your people to suffer even if you could. So King Umb and I, ourselves, will oblige you by making it possible for you to join your beloved subjects. Owing to your high rank as the two most powerful persons in the Land of Oz, we will do you the honor of taking your shapes."

Concluding this triumphant speech, Queen Ra grinned with malicious satisfaction and said gloatingly, "At last the Royal Ozma and the Great Glinda bow to a power greater than their own! Come," she called to King Umb, "you take the form of Glinda, I will take that of Ozma."

With this the Mimic Monarchs advanced on Ozma and Glinda. The little Ruler and Glinda the Good were silent. Both realized that Queen Ra had spoken the truth when she had declared their powers to be useless against the Mimics. Therefore the girl Ruler and the Sorceress made no effort to combat their enemies, but stood bravely and proudly awaiting their fate.

At that very moment when King Umb and Queen Ra were about to seize the shadows of Ozma and Glinda, a small, black form streaked with the speed of light from underneath Ozma's throne straight to the menacing figures of the Mimic King and Queen. It was Toto! With fierce growls and barks he began worrying and snapping at the ankles of the Mimic Monarchs.

The sudden appearance of the little dog and his desperate attack took Ra and Umb completely by surprise. For a moment they entirely forgot Ozma and Glinda and devoted all their efforts to freeing themselves from the snapping jaws of the furiously snarling little dog.

This respite which Toto had so bravely won saved Ozma and Glinda from sharing the fate of their subjects. A few seconds after Toto's attack, there suddenly appeared in the entrance of the throne room three figures, two of whom the Scarecrow joyfully recognized as Dorothy and the Little Wizard. They were accompanied by a maiden who was unknown to the Scarecrow but whose beauty was quite evident. For an instant the trio stood in the doorway, surveying the strange scene that met their eyes in Ozma's Royal Throne Room.

Ozana's Fairy Arts

wiftly Princess Ozana—for the maiden was she—advanced to the center of the throne room. She was followed closely by the Wizard and Dorothy, who bore in her arms the sleeping form of a tiny, white kitten.

At the appearance of Dorothy, Toto stopped worrying the ankles of King Umb and Queen Ra and ran to meet the little girl. So happy was the excited little dog to see his beloved mistress that he even ignored the presence of the sleeping kitten. Dorothy knelt and caressed him.

Meanwhile, Queen Ra, recognizing Ozana, paled and gasped: "The Guardian of Oz!"

"Yes," admitted Ozana calmly, "it is I, Princess Ozana."

King Umb was so terrified at the appearance of the little maiden that the big fellow's knees knocked together and his face turned a sickly, green hue.

But it cannot be said that Queen Ra lacked courage. After the first shock of Ozana's appearance, the Queen summoned her spirits and faced the fairy maid defiantly. Ra had determined not to give up her triumph without a struggle.

Clasping her palms to Dorothy's Magic Belt, the Mimic Queen whispered a command to it. But nothing happened.

Ozana divined what the Queen was about, but she only smiled.

In a rage, Queen Ra tore the useless belt from her waist and flung it to the throne room floor.

"You should know better," Ozana gently chided the infuriated Queen, "than to attempt to work such simple magic on me. Even if you had succeeded in transforming me into a wooden doll, I would still have retained my fairy powers and been able to defeat you."

Fright and realization that she was defeated mingled in Queen Ra's eyes as she stared at Ozana. The unhappy Queen said not a word. She sat spell-bound, gazing with fearful fascination at the serene features of her girlish opponent.

Ozana was speaking with an air of calm justice. "Because I appeared absorbed in my own occupations," she addressed Queen Ra, "you counted me harmless. You believed I would be unaware of your evil-doing. You thought you could attack Oz without my knowing it. But you were wrong. And now the time has come for me to fulfill the trust placed in me by Queen Lurline when she made me Guardian of Oz. At that time she imparted to me the same powers over the race of Mimics that only she, of all fairies, possesses. I shall use those powers as Queen Lurline would wish me to. I shall place her enchantment once more on the Mimics so that they will be powerless to steal the shapes of all who dwell in the Land of Oz. At the same time, the reweaving of this fairy enchantment will release all those Oz people whose shapes are now held by the Mimics."

As Ozana completed this speech, she described a large circle in the air before her with her fairy wand. Immediately that space was filled with a silvery, cloud-like radiance that glowed and shimmered. Then, while Ozma and the rest watched, a scene appeared in the cloud of silver mist. Dorothy and the Wizard recognized it as the interior of the Mimic cavern inside hollow Mount Illuso. Far in the top of the cavern they saw a scarlet spider web, in the center of which squatted a huge crimson spider. While those in the throne room watched with fascinated interest, the spider, seeming to sense that it was being observed, scuttled with a sudden, crab-like motion to the outer edge of the web. There it squatted, its eyes glowing like dull, red coals.

With the tip of her wand, Ozana touched the head of the image of the spider. Instantly, the creature leaped into the air and trembled convulsively, as though it had received an electric shock. Then it began slowly to dissolve before their eyes. First its legs wilted, grew shapeless and melted away. Next its body collapsed inwardly, like an over-ripe melon, finally shriveling and disappearing altogether.

Now the spellbound spectators in the throne room saw a spot of silver light appear on the outermost strand of the crimson web. The light raced over every

coil of the immense web, progressing swiftly to the web's center. As fast as the silver light flashed along the scarlet coils, they vanished. In a few seconds more not a trace remained of the vast web or its loathsome occupant. The point of cleansing silver light winked out; the image of the Mimic cavern faded; and the silver mist vanished from the throne room.

At this same instant, shouts of joy and exchanges of affectionate greetings rang through the Royal Palace and were echoed throughout the Emerald City. The sound of these happy voices told Princess Ozma that her beloved subjects were no longer under the spell of the Mimics. In the throne room itself, the Mimic-Oz people, who had bound the Scarecrow and his companions and brought them before King Umb and Queen Ra, vanished. In their places stood Mimics in their variety of repulsive animal and bird shapes. While the startled Oz people watched, the Mimics flitted and shifted about the Royal Throne Room, changing their forms in the manner peculiar to these creatures.

But for the moment the Mimics were forgotten, as all eyes were fastened with admiration and gratitude on Princess Ozana.

Ozana smiled happily. "Queen Ra," she said, "you are now quite powerless to harm the people of Oz." Queen Ra, who had watched Ozana's fairy magic with fascinated interest, knew she was utterly defeated. All her old arrogance and overbearing manner vanished. With bowed head, she refrained from meeting the eyes of Ozana or those of any of her former victims.

CHAPTER 20
In the Mirrored Ballroom

ow Ozma stepped forward. With happy tears of gratitude sparkling in her eyes, she grasped the hands of Princess Ozana. "How can I ever thank you for what you have done?"

Ozana seemed embarrassed. "The truth is," she admitted, "had I done my duty, as Queen Lurline instructed, and watched the Mimics more closely, the creatures would never have dared to invade Oz. I owe all of you my humblest apology for this neglect of duty. The least I could do," she added soberly, "was to right the wrongs already committed."

"Well," said Dorothy happily, "all's well that ends well, and we think you're fine, Ozana."

"Thank you, my dear," smiled Ozana, affectionately stroking the little girl's hair.

"I think we owe Toto a great debt of thanks," observed the wise Glinda. "Had it not been for the little dog's bravery, you and I, Ozma, would have undergone the unpleasant experience of becoming Mimic victims."

"You are right," agreed Ozma, turning to the dog. "I had not forgotten your brave action, Toto. Nothing Glinda and I can say or do will properly reward you. Nevertheless I shall have made for you a handsome new collar studded with emeralds and bearing your name in gold letters as a slight token of our gratitude."

"Thank you, your Highness," said Toto shyly. "It was nothing, really. When I saw the big birds stealing the shapes of Trot and Betsy and Button Bright and all the others out in the garden, I was frightened so I ran and hid under your throne. I could peep out and see everything that was going on, and when the Mimic King and Queen threatened you and Glinda I became so angry that I just forgot about everything else."

"Good dog! " said the Wizard, patting Toto's head.

Dorothy beamed proudly at her little pet.

"Dear me!" exclaimed Ozma, gazing at the Mimics in the throne room. "How are we ever to transport all these creatures to their cavern home? We can't have them here to overrun Oz, even though they are now harmless," she added, shuddering with revulsion at the shifting shapes of evil assumed by the Mimics.

"That is simple," said Ozana. "Is there a room in the palace with a great many mirrors?"

"Yes," replied Ozma, "the Grand Ballroom which adjoins the throne room—its walls and ceiling are composed entirely of mirrors."

"Then let us go to the ballroom," said Ozana.

Ozma and Glinda led Ozana to the entrance of the Grand Ballroom. Dorothy and the Wizard and Toto followed.

Ozana paused before the great door which was flung wide open. In her bell-like voice she murmured the words of a powerful fairy spell. Immediately King Umb and Queen Ra, followed by the other Mimics in the throne room, advanced as though they were in a trance to the portal of the mirrored ballroom. Then they passed into the room itself. Ozana continued to chant her fairy spell. Now came a whole procession of the Mimic creatures, first from all over the Royal Palace and finally from every part of the Emerald City. They came trooping in by the hundreds, wearing a myriad of fantastic shapes and forms. At length the very last Mimic had entered the ballroom, and, huge though the room was, it seemed to the onlookers that it must surely be filled to overflowing with the Mimic horde.

By this time, the Scarecrow, Scraps, Tik-Tok and the rest who had been bound with ropes by the Mimics were freed and they with Trot, Cap'n Bill, Betsy Bobbin, Button Bright and the others all crowded about the entrance to look curiously into the ballroom. Even the Cowardly Lion, the Hungry Tiger and Hank the Mule crowded into the throne room. The three beasts had awakened from the sleep cast on them by Queen Ra when Ozana had re-woven the spell that protected the Oz inhabitants.

"Why," rumbled the Cowardly Lion, "the room's empty!"

In a sense the lion was right. There was no one in the Grand Ballroom, it was true. But Dorothy and the others could plainly see the flitting, shifting shadow shapes of the Mimics in the mirrors that paneled the walls and ceiling of the great room—shadow creatures caught and confined in the depths of the mirrors!

"I wonder," Dorothy whispered, "what will become of them."

CHAPTER 21

The Shattering of the Mirrors

ow we can send the Mimics back to Mount Illuso at will," said Ozana in answer to Dorothy's question. "All we need to do is shatter the mirrors and the Mimics will return to their gloomy realm, banished forever from Oz."

It was Ozma who followed Ozana's suggestion and brought about the breaking of the mirrors. The dainty ruler lifted her wand and murmured a fairy charm. Instantly every mirror in the Grand Ballroom shivered and shattered with a vast, tinkling sound. Not one of the scores of mirrors in the great chamber was left whole.

"It would be too bad," Ozana remarked, "to mar permanently the beauty of your lovely ballroom." She lifted her wand, and while the onlookers blinked the mirrors were whole again. In their gleaming depths was no trace of the Mimic horde. The Grand Ballroom was as splendid as ever.

As it was now nearing noon, Ozma graciously invited Ozana to join her and Glinda with Dorothy and the Wizard, Aunt Em, Trot, Cap'n Bill, Betsy Bobbin, Button Bright, the Scarecrow, Scraps and others of her friends for luncheon in the dining room of her own Royal Suite.

Dorothy and the Wizard related their adventures on Mount Illuso, and then the Scarecrow tried to make clear to Ozma, Glinda and Dorothy and the Wizard everything that had happened in the Emerald City during their absence. Scraps helped him out, and Betsy Bobbin reminded him of things he had forgotten, while Trot chimed in, and Button Bright wanted to tell the story his way. There was such a chatter it was a wonder Ozma and the rest understood anything.

Just as the meal was about to end, there was a knock on the door and Uncle Henry breathlessly entered the room. After Aunt Em and Dorothy had hugged and kissed Uncle Henry, Dorothy told him how she had got back to the Emerald City. (He had read an account of the rest of her adventures in Glinda's Great Book of Records the night before.) Scraps, helped out by Aunt Em, filled in the details of what had happened in the palace since he and the Sawhorse had left.

When they had finished, Uncle Henry exhibited several sheets of paper closely filled with writing.

The Shattering of the Mirrors

"Here's the whole story of the Mimics: I copied every-thing the Great Book of Records had to say about 'em, and then I left Glinda's Castle last night, travelin' all night long so as to get here as early today as possible. But I guess," he concluded, gazing ruefully at the papers he carried, "these ain't much use anymore."

"Not one of us could have done better than you did, Uncle Henry," Ozma consoled him. "Instead of regret-ting your trip," she added wisely, "Let us instead be grateful that there is no longer any need for us to con-cern ourselves with what the Great Book of Records has to say about the Mimics."

Glinda announced that she must return to her Castle in the Quadling Country, from which she had been absent too long. Bidding goodbye to all her friends, the Great Sorceress was transported in the twinkling of an eye by her magic art to her far-away Castle. With Glinda's departure the rest of Ozma's guests began to take their leave, until finally the Girl Ruler was alone with only Dorothy and Ozana. Ozma had noticed that throughout the merry luncheon, Ozana had appeared quiet and subdued, as though she were deeply occupied with thoughts of her own.

"Tell me," Ozma said gently, taking Princess Ozana's hand in her own, "is there something troubling you, my dear?"

With a smile, Ozana replied, "Yes, Ozma, there is. Truthfully, I dread returning to lonely Mount Illuso. In the short time I have been privileged to enjoy the companionship of Dorothy and the Wizard, and the society of the Oz people here in the Emerald City, I have come to realize more than ever what a terribly lonely life I lead on Mount Illuso. And," she added, gazing affectionately at Dorothy, "I have become very fond of little Dorothy. I shall be very sorry indeed to leave her and all the rest of you for that forsaken mountain top."

Ozma laughed softly. "Everyone loves our Princess Dorothy. But," and the Little Ruler's expression grew serious as she continued, "I sympathize with you, Ozana. Perhaps there is a way out of your predicament. Is there any real reason why you should return to Mount Illuso? The Mimics are harmless enough now. We can follow their actions in the Magic Picture and the Great Book of Records. And you can use your fairy powers to control the Mimics from the Land of Oz as easily as you could from the top of Mount Illuso."

"You mean—?" exclaimed Ozana eagerly.

"That we would like nothing better than to have you make your home here in the Land of Oz," said Ozma warmly. "Furthermore it is my belief that through your long years of lonely vigil on Mount Illuso, and your courageous rescue of the people of Oz from the Mimics, you have more than earned a home in Oz."

"Oh, Ozma, thank you!" exclaimed Ozana. And then she added doubtfully, "Do you think Queen Lurline will give her consent?"

"I see no reason why she should not," answered Ozma. "It so happens that I am to speak with Queen Lurline within the hour. We made arrangements to confer this afternoon on some important happenings in the great outside world. During our conversation I will ask her about your remaining in Oz."

"Thank you, Ozma," murmured Ozana. "I can't begin to tell you how grateful I am."

"Now if you will excuse me," said Ozma, "I must prepare to establish communication with Queen Lurline."

Arm in arm, Dorothy and Ozana made their way to Dorothy's rooms, where they spent the next hour in conversation. Dorothy was well pleased with the prospect of Ozana's making her home in Oz, for she believed the Princess would be a delightful companion.

At last there came a gentle rap on the door, and Princess Ozma entered Dorothy's room.

Ozana and Dorothy rose to their feet and looked questioningly at Ozma.

"It is all settled," the Girl Ruler announced with her brightest smile. "Queen Lurline readily gave her consent. From this moment on, dear cousin, you are no longer Ozana of Mount Illuso, but Ozana, Princess of Oz."

CHAPTER 22

What the Magic Picture Revealed

After the first happy excitement over Ozma's news had subsided Ozana grew serious and Dorothy thought she detected a note of sadness in the Fairy Maid's voice as she said:

"There is one duty I must perform, Ozma, before I can begin my new existence as an inhabitant of your lovely fairyland."

"What is that?" asked Ozma.

"I must restore the pine folk and their village to their original forms, as part of the Pine Forest that covers the top of Mount Illuso. Likewise, Story Blossom Garden must be returned to its original state, that is, ordinary wild flowers blossoming in the forest."

"Why must you do that?" asked Dorothy.

"Since I am not to return to Mount Illuso, the pine folk and the garden are left entirely to the mercy of the Mimics and other wicked creatures who dwell in the Land of the Phanfasms. Quick transformation of the mountain top to its original state is far better than destruction of the village and the garden by creatures of evil."

Ozana's voice was tinged with real regret. "Ozma, may I look into your Magic Picture to see the garden and the village just once more, before I cause them to vanish forever?"

Ozma made no reply other than to nod and lead the way to her boudoir where hung the Magic Picture. Dorothy was mystified by the expression on the Little Ruler's face. She was sure Ozma was repressing a smile and was secretly amused at something.

On the way to Ozma's boudoir, Dorothy, who had grown fond of Felina the White Kitten, asked, "What about Felina, Ozana? Did you find her on Mount Illuso?"

"No, indeed," Ozana explained. "Felina accompanied me when I first went to Mount Illuso. She is my own pet. She is a fairy kitten and is as old as I am and that is many hundreds of years."

Standing before the Magic Picture, Ozana said quietly, "I wish to see the Story Blossom Garden on Mount Illuso."

Chapter Twenty-Two

Instantly the Magic Picture's familiar country scene faded. In its place appeared, not the lovely Story Blossom Garden, but a barren, desert waste. Even the blue pond had disappeared. There was no sign of any living thing in the dreary, desert scene.

"What can it mean?" Dorothy cried. "Ozma, do you think something's gone wrong with the Magic Picture?"

Ozana paled slightly and her eyes were troubled as she spoke again, "I wish to see the Village of Pineville on Mount Illuso."

This time the Magic Picture shifted only slightly to show a second expanse of gray wasteland as gloomy and forbidding as the first.

"They are gone," cried Ozana in dismay. "The garden and the village are gone!"

What the Magic Picture Revealed

To the amazement of Ozana and Dorothy, Ozma met their consternation by laughing merrily.

"Of course they are gone," the Little Ruler said, "because they are here!"

"What do you mean?" asked Ozana.

"First of all," began Ozma, "you didn't think, did you, Ozana, that no matter how much we wanted you to make your home with us, we would ask you to sacrifice your lovely Story Blossom Garden and the quaint people of your Village of Pineville? Queen Lurline and I discussed this matter seriously and agreed we could not permit the garden and the village to be destroyed. So, after I finished my conversation with Queen Lurline, I consulted a map of the Land of Oz prepared by Professor Woggle Bug and found just what I was looking for a small mountain in the Quadling Country, only a short distance to the south from the Emerald City and not far from Miss Cutenclip's interesting village. The top of this mountain was about the same in area as the top of Mount Illuso, and it was an uninhabited sandy waste. While you and Dorothy talked, I worked a powerful fairy spell that transported the Pine Forest, the Village of Pineville and the Story Blossom Garden to the Oz mountain top. Hereafter that mountain will be known as Story Blossom Mountain. That is why my Magic Picture showed only a desert waste when you asked to see the pine village and the Story Blossom Garden on Mount Illuso, The Magic Picture couldn't show them to you on Mount Illuso for they are no longer there!"

What the Magic Picture Revealed

"Instead," Ozma concluded, "they are here in the Land of Oz." Turning to the Magic Picture, she said, "I wish to see Story Blossom Garden on Story Blossom Mountain."

The image of the desert waste faded and in the frame of the Magic Picture appeared the beautiful fairy garden. The vision was so real that Dorothy could almost hear the blossoms whispering among themselves.

Bright tears of joy and gratitude sparkled in Ozana's violet eyes.

"What happened to Hi-Lo and his elevator?" Dorothy asked.

"They were transported, too," replied Ozma quickly.

"I imagine," the Girl Ruler went on, "that Hi-Lo will be a very busy little man, carrying visitors up and down in his elevator. And you, Ozana, will be able to live in your pretty cottage and work in your wonderful garden without fear of ever becoming lonely. Every day will bring you visitors from the Emerald City and all parts of the Land of Oz who will be eager to see the pine folk and their village and to enjoy Story Blossom Garden. Really, Ozana, it is we who are indebted to you," Ozma concluded.

Dorothy beamed lovingly at Ozma. Then, turning to Ozana, the little girl said, "Now I guess you understand, Ozana, why you're just about the luckiest person in the whole world to be invited to live in the Land of Oz."

The Grand Banquet

The next day was given over entirely to welcoming Ozana to Oz. Early in the morning, the Sawhorse was hitched to the Red Wagon, and a merry company of travelers rode out of the Emerald City to be the first visitors to Story Blossom Mountain. In the front seat of the Red Wagon rode Ozma, Ozana, Dorothy and Trot. In the rear seat were Betsy Bobbin, Cap'n Bill, the Wizard and the Scarecrow.

The Sawhorse needed no reins to guide him, as this intelligent horse responded to spoken commands. Being tireless and having no need for oats or water, he was in many ways superior to ordinary horses. As the Red Wagon pulled up near the entrance to Hi-Lo's elevator, the party was met by flaxen-haired Miss

---

201

The Grand Banquet

Cuttenclip. Not far distant was a pretty little paper village of paper people, ruled over by Miss Cuttenclip, who had skillfully cut out the entire village and all its inhabitants from "live" paper furnished her by Glinda the Good. Ozma had communicated with Miss Cuttenclip before the journey, inviting her to meet them and visit Story Blossom Mountain and afterwards to accompany them to the Emerald City for the Grand Banquet to be given that evening in Ozana's honor. Ozana and Miss Cuttenclip became friends at once.

Hi-Lo greeted Ozana and the rest joyfully, but it was necessary for him to make two trips to carry this large party to the mountain top. Ozana showed the visitors around the Village of Pineville and Story Blossom Garden. On the surface of the blue pond floated the three swans. Knowing that Ozana would no longer need them to carry her back to Mount Illuso, Ozma had thoughtfully transported the swans from the courtyard of her palace to their pond when she had worked the fairy spell that had brought the Story Blossom Garden to Oz.

After passing several happy hours in the Story Blossom Garden, Ozana and her guests returned to the bottom of the mountain, where the Sawhorse and the Red Wagon waited to carry them back to the Emerald City.

The rest of the day was devoted to preparing for the Grand Banquet to be given in Ozana's honor that evening in the Grand Dining Room of the Royal Palace. All of Ozma's old friends and companions were invited.

Late in the afternoon the guests began arriving. The Tin Woodman journeyed from his glittering Tin Castle in the Winkie Country. Jack Pumpkinhead left his house, a huge, hollowed-out pumpkin in the middle of a pumpkin field. The Highly Magnified and Thoroughly Educated Woggle Bug traveled from the Royal Athletic College of Oz, of which he was Principal.

Among other guests who came from great distances were Glinda the Good, the Giant Frogman, Cayke the Cookie Cook, Dr. Pipt—the Crooked Magician who was no longer crooked nor a magician, his wife Margolotte, the Good Witch of the North and Lady Aurex Queen of the Skeezers.

Dorothy transported all of these visitors to the Emerald City by means of her Magic Belt, except Glinda, who arrived by her own magic.

Chapter Twenty-Three

The Grand Banquet proved to be one of the most brilliant and delightful occasions ever to be enjoyed in the Emerald City, and was long remembered by all who were present. In addition to the delicious food, there was music and special entertainment for the guests. The Scarecrow made a gallant speech of welcome to which Ozana charmingly replied. The Woggle Bug could not be restrained from reading an "Ode to Ozana," which he claimed he had composed on the spur of the moment, writing it on the cuff of his shirt sleeve. A number of the guests thought the composition sounded suspiciously like an "Ode to Ozma," which the Woggle Bug had written some years before, but they were all too kind-hearted to mention this. The Tin Woodman sang a love song, which he had written especially for the occasion, and which he had titled "You're My Tin Type." While the song was only moderately good, the Tin Woodman sang in a metallic tenor with great feeling and the company applauded politely.

Then the Little Wizard made them all gasp with a truly wonderful display of magic. The Wizard opened his show by causing a fountain of many colored flames of fire to appear in the center of the banquet table. At his command, streamers of fire of different colors— red, green, blue, rose, orange, violet—leaped out from the burning fountain to touch the unlighted candles that stood at the place of each guest. After this the fountain of fire vanished while the now-lighted candles continued to burn throughout the banquet, each shedding the light imparted to it by the colored fire.

Chapter Twenty-Three

The Wizard concluded his entertainment by tossing a napkin into the air above the banquet table. Instantly the napkin disappeared and a storm of confetti showered down on the guests, while band after band of what appeared to be brightly colored paper ribbon fell over the party. But it didn't take Button Bright long to discover and announce with shouts of glee to the rest of the guests, that the confetti and the many colored paper ribbons were really the most delicious of spearmint, peppermint, clove, licorice, lime, lemon, orange and chocolate candies and mints. This, of course, provided the perfect ending for the dinner.

At the table occupied by the animals, there was a great deal of talking and merry-making. Toto received many compliments on his handsome new red leather collar, embellished with clusters of emeralds and his own name in solid gold letters. Princess Ozma, herself, had fitted the collar about the proud little dog's neck that very afternoon as a tribute to Toto's loyalty and bravery.

The Grand Banquet

Just as the happy banquet was about to end, Toto, who had been so absorbed in all the excitement and the Wizard's marvelous tricks, that he had scarcely tasted his food, turned to his bowl of milk. He found the tiny White Kitten Felina daintily lapping the last of the milk from the bowl with her little, pink tongue.

Toto sniffed. "I never could understand," he growled, "what it is that witches and fairies and little girls see in cats!"

Tote's Blemished Blossom

[Retrofit Edition Content]

written by
ADAM NICOLAI

illustrated by
ARDIAN HODA

www.empty-grave.com

Tote's Blemished Blossom

Our story begins with a well-traveled grain of pollen, delivered by the trade winds of Ev to a clearing in the great pine forest atop Mt. Illuso.

In its descent, the microscopic red spec drifted along the streets of Pineville and through the white-enameled slats of a fence surrounding the Story Blossom Garden. It flitted uncertainly amongst the myriads of eager flowers—whose petals quivered at the prospect of telling their tales—before arriving at its final destination—the tip of a hair in the left nostril of the nose of Fairy Princess Ozana—creator of the garden, the town, and all its residents, and, of course, the distant cousin of Princess Ozma, the supreme ruler of the neighboring country of Oz.

The pine-scented breeze mussed Ozana's golden hair as she poked about the flower beds. She tucked the stray strands behind her ears.

"Oh! I choose you!"

Ozana plucked a pristine white Oleander blossom from its stem and sniffed it. The arrangement of the petals made it appear almost as if the flower had a face—a face that fluttered with delight at being chosen. In a big-bellied grandad's voice, the Oleander spoke:

You won't be disappointed, milady. Mine is the timeless tale of a beautiful maiden whisked away from the dreary doldrums of her life by none other than her One True Love.

"That sounds simply wonderful," said Ozana. She held the blossom up to her ear. "Please, do begin."

The Oleander gave a polite little cough then started in.

Long ago and far away, in the illustrious Palace of Banal, lived a princess named—

"Ah!" Ozana held the blossom at arm's length.

Ahem. There lived a little princ—

"Ah!" She looked with blank eyes out at the sun filtering through the pines and held a finger to the flower's mouthish petals.

Well, I never! Interruptions and then shushing? This is—

"ACHOO!"

Ozana was suddenly overcome by a fit of sneezing, much of which was directed right in the flower's faux face. Its petals were wet and drooping when the outburst finally subsided.

"I am *so* sorry my dear blossom!" Ozana gently patted it with the hem of her skirt. "I don't know what—"

The Oleander was silent.

Ozana watched in confusion as its delicate petals shriveled up, turning from white to grey to mushy brown. She set the withered blossom down and just stared at it. "Most unusual," she said to herself.

Tote's Blemished Blossom

Ozana looked out over the colorful sea of flowers. "Dolly!" She shouted, cupping her hands over her mouth. "Dolly! I need you!"

A poppy bed—tightly packed with blossoms of every color imaginable—rustled and, with two grunts and a bit of mumbling, the top of a head rose just above the flowers. Its shiny painted-on bonnet paused then bobbed out toward the garden path.

A shortish young woman emerged from between the wall of stems and stiffly brushed clumps of mud from her apron—which was nothing more than a thin coat of white-enamel paint atop the slightly thicker blue paint of her dress. Only she and her creator knew what was beneath the dress, be it a layer of the same pinkish skin as her face or just bare wood—a fine-grained white pine.

"Yes, Princess Ozana—" The wooden woman trotted down the mulched path. "—I'm coming."

"Oh, Dolly," said Ozana as her faithful maid drew near, "something odd has just occurred."

"Ma'am?"

"Have you ever heard of a Story Blossom going—unheard?"

"Ma'am, I'm not sure what you—" The maid looked where Ozana was looking—the contorted, sapless flower on the ground.

"This wonderful Oleander was beginning its tale when I had a bit of a sneeze—" Ozana poked at the remains. "It withered as all spent stories do—but *before* its story was told!"

"My, my," Dolly said, kneeling down for a closer look, "I've never heard a story *not* tell itself."

They sat and were collectively pondering this unlikely occurrence when a cat—that would have been wonderfully white had it not been covered whisker to tail in rich, black dirt—bounded out from the daisies and stumbled uncertainly down the path toward Ozana and Dolly. The cat sat between them, sniffed the rotten blossom, swatted at it twice, and—with a saucy flick of her tail—began drunkenly nuzzling into the hem of Ozana's dress.

"Felina!" Ozana laughed, gently nudging the cat away with her foot. "Oh, I know where *you've* been, you dirty kitty."

Felina rolled on her back and shamelessly displayed her belly, which was caked with mud and the remnants of catnip petals.

"Perhaps Dolly could be persuaded to give you a bath, hmm?"

"Yes, ma'am." The maid grimaced as Ozana turned, collected her dress about her, and started back down the path to the cottage.

"Oh and Dolly—" Ozana said over her shoulder. "—please keep an eye on that defective Oleander and let me know if anything else out of the ordinary happens. We can't have some unknown affliction running amuck amongst my Story Blossoms now can we?"

"No, ma'am." Dolly prodded the remains of the story-less blossom. The little maid wondered if the tale was still there somewhere in that sticky brown mess

or if it would remain unheard forever—if unheard stories ever really existed in the first place. And as Felina rubbed up against Dolly's back she wondered why *she* was always the one washing the cat.

"Ma'am, ma'am, ma'am," she muttered, carefully covering the dead Oleander over with dirt.

* * *

Creeping through the shadows of night, Dolly darted from bush to bush until she spied her target—a still, boyish form leaning into the pine siding of Ozana's cottage. He was standing next to a window that threw a warm yellow glow out as far as the dark allowed it to go.

Dolly's breath was shallow and ragged. Her paring knife dimly reflected the light when she angled the blade just so. She clenched the hilt in her teeth like a pirate then elbow-crawled silently through the cool, dewy grasses.

Dolly came up behind the motionless figure. She glanced in the window—then deftly jammed her knife in the side of his head.

"Oh, Tote," she whispered, her breath hot on the back of his neck, "I'm sorry."

She stabbed again and again, wrenching the handle up and down with each blow.

"So, so, so sorry, you old lug."

The boy did not move.

Dolly licked her finger, stuck it in the jaggy hole she had just cut, and swished it around.

Tote's Blemished Blossom

"I drag you all the way out here. Then I remember I forgot the carver. Then—ditsy me—I forgot to remember to make your ears!"

Dolly pivoted the boy on his heel until he faced her. She winced. "Oh my. It seems I also neglected to give you a 'good side'."

The boy could have passed for one of the Pine Folk had he not been lumpy, lopsided, disproportionate, unsymmetrical, and just plain wrong-looking. Although he would have made a very *right-looking* monster.

A cheerful whistling came from inside the cottage. She peeked in the window, quickly positioned herself so she wouldn't be seen, then held the knife at Tote's throat.

"Now don't you start distracting me, my friend. I'm going to catch the trick tonight. I can feel it."

Inside, Ozana hummed as she danced graceful circles around a perfectly-carved, unpainted, pine girl. The girl showed no reaction as Ozana's blades skimmed her skin, throwing paper-thin shavings to the air in a flurry of glinting steel.

The Fairy Princess stopped, set down the knives, and ran her fingertips lightly over the girl's body. "Just right," she said. "Now for the pinch of life."

Dolly braced herself and focused on Ozana's hands, perfectly mimicking every flourish, flick, and twitch on her own. She held her breath. Dolly knew she needed to nail that final pinch if she wanted any hope of making a friend.

Suddenly, Felina jumped up on the inner window-sill and looked the peeper straight in the eye. Dolly was so startled she fell backwards, pulling Tote on top of her.

In seconds, she squirmed out from under the boy, propped him back up against the cottage, and was giving Felina the 'it's bath time' look. Felina hissed and smeared a gooey nose-print in the fog on the glass. Then she hopped from the sill and curled up in a cozy-looking ball in front of the fireplace.

When Dolly got situated she saw that the moment had escaped her yet again. "Oh *root-worms*," she said, spitting on the pine siding.

The wooden girl inside was moving about the room, examining everything with great curiosity. She paused at a rough-cut log table and marveled at the dozens of jars of paint and brushes. Ozana and the girl chatted enthusiastically, fawning over their favorite colors of paint.

The Fairy Princess dipped a brush in bright, green enamel, slopped it on the girl's bare wood shoes and spread it around. The girl picked up a larger brush and began painting pink polka-dots on her soon-to-be-green dress.

Dolly scowled and elbowed Tote in the chest. She had tried every hand movement and fairy gesture she could recall—pinching his nose, plucking his chin, poking his eyes, and rubbing his cheeks—but nothing happened. Tote remained still as a statue.

"Oh well, Tote. I had my hopes but it looks like you won't be the one after all. I did try, though. I'm sure you saw I tried."

She tipped him over, grabbed an ankle with each hand, and—leaving a long rut in the grass—pulled him to the edge of a dense wall of towering pines. Dolly took a deep breath, hunched forward, and began the long drag through the woods. She decided to stop naming her creations before bringing them to life— she was running out of names.

* * *

Dolly's hands moved expertly, making perfect furrows in the loose dirt. She dropped a spent, withered, Carnation in the hole and spread a thin blanket of fertile earth over it.

"Well *that* was a pleasant story," she said. "I wonder if there will be a sequel."

She continued down the rows, pruning stubby leaves and imperfections, evicting pesky grubs and aphids, and listening to pitch after pitch as the blossoms tried to sell themselves to anyone with ears and a moment of free time.

At the end of the row was a flower that made Dolly gasp.

"Ack! What in root-rot are you?" She poked at the odd plant with her pruning-shears. She'd never seen anything even remotely like it before.

If Dolly was forced to say something nice about it she would surely have been at a loss for words. She couldn't fathom so much *wrong* in the same place at the same time.

The stem was gnarled and the leaves misshapen and twisted—each one its own special brand of ugly. The blossoms, if they could be called that, were amorphous, about as colorful as dried blood, and exuded a pungent mix of black licorice and sulfurous fumes.

The strangest thing, though, was that this particular bloomer was silent—dead quiet in a garden where *every* blossom had a tale to tell.

"Hello?" Dolly flicked the stem. "Anything you want to tell me?"

Nothing. Perhaps the blossoms hadn't fully bloomed.

Then she remembered she was right around the spot where the Oleander blossom had fallen victim to the royal snot of Princess Ozana.

"Aha! So you're *that* one!" She leaned in close. "But if you're speechless now, and were interrupted last time, where did your story go? Hmm Mr. Creepy-Bud? What happened to it?"

Despite the appalling aesthetics, Dolly took an instant liking to the botanical abomination. It made her think of all her almost-friends except—unlike them—the plant was actually alive. She also found the experience of being around a *quiet* flower unexpectedly refreshing.

"Now Ozana explicitly told me to let her know if you turned out to be—*unusual*." Dolly stroked one of its leaves. It felt like velvet going one way but was prickly and very near burning the other way.

"I'll find a pot and dig you up right now. If your unusualness *is* contagious Ozana certainly wouldn't want you spreading it around." Dolly stood up, her knees creaking in protest, and an almost imperceptible flake of flesh-colored paint peeled away at her ankle. "Ozana likes to have everything just so—and entirely as expected."

* * *

Dolly sighed as she gazed at the abnormal plant firmly packed in its wood pot. During the transplant she found the roots had been just as unusual as everything else. The bright-red mess of tangly confusion looked like spaghetti gone awry. The individual roots seemed to have their own personalities as well. Some were bashful and shied away from her touch while others lashed out aggressively—wrapping around her fingers like pythons on their dinners.

"Alright then. Off we go to the Great Fairy Princess Ozana. I'm sure you'll like her. She makes everything perfect—you'll get fixed up in a jiff."

Dolly looked at the plant—its spoiled-meat blossoms, motley assortment of leaves, and the stem all caught up in its own kinks and gnarls instead of gracefully arcing about like flowers should. The plant was *certainly* different.

"Hmm," Dolly said, "you *clearly* don't belong but I think I prefer you the way you are." She turned the pot, amazed at how no two blossoms or leaves were the same—no matter what angle she looked from.

"In fact, we won't go see Ozana after all. I think I'll keep you to myself." She smiled and hugged the pot. "I even know the *perfect* place to plant you!"

Dolly tossed the flower over the white-enameled fence then climbed over herself, losing a bit of elbow paint to the pickets and—ironically—getting a good-sized splinter in her wooden thumb in the process.

"After all, if Ozana really *wanted* something like you she would have *made* something like you. But here in Pineville the people are all sanded smooth and the Oleanders in the Garden are always perfectly Oleanderish."

Dolly whistled an off-key ditty and stepped amongst the trees—the unusual plant clutched tight to her white-pine chest.

* * *

"There you go." Dolly tossed the empty pot aside and tamped down the loose dirt around the base of the plant atop the mound.

"Tote," she whispered, on her knees and with her face down close to the raised dirt, "I hope you enjoy your new friend—that is if there is enough 'you' there to do some enjoying."

Dolly scanned the gathering of graves. "I'm sorry I don't have something for each of you. Tote was the closest to *being*—" She shrugged. "Maybe this plant will make some more of itself. Then there would be enough to go around."

She noticed the darkening sky and knew full well Ozana would soon be looking for her. She set off back

through the trees—daydreaming of a forest brimming with abnormal plants and townfuls of unexpectedly imperfect people.

* * *

Tote wondered why *strange happenings* always seemed to take place in the dead of night. And underground. And with the muffled *pit-pat-ploop* of raindrops hitting the dirt above him.

Wait. *WHAT!?*

Tote *wondered* how he came to be *wondering*. Then he wondered how he could wonder about wondering. He was dead.

Well, technically he was unalive. To be dead he had to have been alive at some point. Tote never was. In fact, he had always prided himself on being a model example of unliving. And yet here he lay...

It was the Night of the Living Unalive.

A hand burst up from the ground. Then another. The clawed fingers searched for purchase in the mud, found it, and strained to haul everything else up.

Dolly's odd plant leaned awkwardly as the earth beneath it bulged and broke. The rain knocked bits of clinging dirt from its roots as it ascended—a botanical messiah.

In a flash of lightning and with a muffled groan, Tote stood up. Clods of earth fell from his body as he stretched his arms and shook his legs. A gooey mash of pine-pulp, sap, and mud oozed from his mouth and ran down his chest.

"Brrr—aaaiiinnnsss—" He moaned. "—Torrrmmmsss?"

The thunder sounded, sending such a shudder through his body it left his rotted teeth chattering. "Brrr," he said again, shivering. "Rain? Storms?"

The rain fell faster and harder. Large mud clumps on his shoulders calved like dirty icebergs—their quarters and thirds and halves washed away. The deep-down earth must have drank too much because the water was doing more pooling than soaking-in—turning his empty grave to a swimming hole.

Awkwardly contorting his body, Tote freed himself from the mud-suction and lurched toward a mid-sized pine that was exposed by lightning. He clung to the slick trunk like a cicada husk.

The torrent abated. Tote relaxed his grip as the solid mass of falling water separated back into individual droplets. He slumped down with his back against the comforting solidity of the tree and tried to piece together a picture of his surroundings from what was revealed in flashes of lightning—a crowd of stalwart pines standing vigil over half-a-dozen mounds suspiciously similar to the one Tote had just emerged from. He wondered if there were other unalive folks and if any of them had caught the living bug as well—maybe it was contagious.

"Hello?" Tote shouted as loud as he could. "Is anyone there?"

Nothing.

Probably couldn't hear him over the storm. Heck, he couldn't even hear himself. Or the rain. Or the thunder. Or, as he was coming to realize, much of anything at all.

Tote figured his ears were plugged with mud like all his other nooks and crannies so he gave his fingers the unpleasant task of dredging them out. The fingers came back empty-handed. His hands also came back empty-handed—feeling nothing remotely ear-like. Tote had *no* ears.

There was just a jaggy hole that had what felt like thin, tangled-up, al dente worms coming out of it. He ran his hands over his face and the rest of his head and discovered similar bunches of firm tubules boring into, or out of, his skull—all tracing back to a snarled nest on his left shoulder. Further probing yielded a crooked stem. Leaves and slimy petals stuck to his hands like paper-mache, confirming his suspicion—a parasitic flower had glommed on to him when he was unliving and under the ground.

Nausea struck when he realized the invasive roots had probably wheedled their way through his entire head. Tote rubbed his chin, weighing his options. He plucked at an unexpected and ingrown beard hair, caught it between thumb and forefinger, and gave it a little tug.

Tote felt like his brain was a tangled ball of twine and pulling that free end had loosened *some* spots but knotted others up tight.

It didn't hurt, per se. The moment of vertigo he felt was more *unusual* than uncomfortable. What *was* uncomfortable was the thought of something drilling

in his shoulder and coming out his chin. He clawed his face and snapped individual roots off at their base.

The rain turned to drizzle. He found the stem and two-handed it, checked his grip, took a deep breath, and pulled with everything his little wooden arms could give. Tote was rewarded with an overwhelming sensation of release.

Then he blacked out.

* * *

Tote awoke to find mud from the previous night had turned into a hard, dry crust covering his whole body. When he sat up it cracked and broke away and revealed to him a world that wrung his insides like a wet dish rag. Oh, the *beauty*!

His gaze followed the thick trunk of a majestic pine up to where the rich green needles of all the trees collided—breaking only in places offering perfect views of the brilliant blue sky. A pillar of mid-afternoon sun had thrust through one of those breaks and cast a warm spotlight on Tote like he was the lead in some grand performance.

A matted blanket of brown and browning pine-needles spread out all around him and as he was running his hands over it to revel in the muted textures he came across something with an oddly familiar feel. He picked it up.

The plant he held before him—limp-blossomed, broken-stemmed, and well-withered—made the rest of the forest look like a washed-out, grey wasteland. The attraction was instant and intense. Tote couldn't imagine there was *anything* in the world more wonderful than what he currently held.

The roots were a lifeless tangle of thin, bright red that glistened in the sun like hair. Tote realized that *they* must have been what was burrowing into him beneath the earth.

"Was it you," he shouted, "wriggling through me underground?"

Tote could have sworn he saw the tip of one of the roots move ever so slightly.

"Because if it was you—" He said, closing his eyes and tightening his hold on the plant, "—I want to thank you! Thank you, thank you!"

He held it close to his chest in a long but cautious hug then gently kissed each of the droopy, near-rotten blossoms.

"I am absolutely *honored* that, of all the things you could have taken root to, you chose me!"

Suddenly, one of the blossoms became a shade of sickly brown, crinkled up, and dropped off the plant.

"Oh!" He said, slapping his head. "Stupid me! You probably can't be laying around with your naked roots flapping in the air. Let me get you back in the ground!"

He rushed to the remains of his grave—a pitted, mostly washed-out mound—and frantically dug. "Oh you'll *love* it. You can stretch your roots and wiggle them all around in the—" He slowed digging then stopped altogether. "—dirt?"

Tote held the plant up to his face. "But maybe you *won't* like it. If you did you probably wouldn't have taken root in my head when there was all that dirt right there. Am I right?"

Nothing.

"I thought all you growy things ate dirt. Don't you need to eat dirt?" He asked.

Nothing.

"Well then, that's settled. The most glorific, leaftacular thing to ever grow, or be, needs—me!"

Tote carefully balanced the plant on his head. Red, red roots dangled before his eyes like beaded curtains. He stood very, *very* still.

"There ya go little buddy! Have at it!" Tote waited a minute then took a tentative step. The plant slid off the back of his head and when it hit the ground the stem crimped and nearly folded over on itself like a *V*.

"Sorry, sorry, sorry," he said. "You must need more time." He arranged the collapsed plant atop his head again and figured he wouldn't move until he felt some indication the spectacular leafster had latched on. So he waited.

And waited.

And waited.

* * *

"Flimdippity!" Tote shouted. "I can't just turn into a *statue*. Now that I *can* move about I think moving about is *implied* and such."

"You are incredible beyond words. We can't stand in one place when people should see how wonderful you are. The whole world needs to see you!"

Out of the corner of his eye, Tote spied Dolly's discarded wood pot, that was half-buried in a neighboring grave by the storm. He gently lifted the plant from his head and set it on the ground. "Don't go anywhere. I have—an *idea*."

Tote put a thin layer of dirt in the bottom of the pot. He scratched his head a moment then started feeling around under the pine needles.

"Yip-yip-yipee!" He pulled a flat, jagged-edged stone from the ground like an arrowhead from an animal hide. Then he ran his finger over the sharpest side. "I hope I'm right because this is bound to sting a little."

Tote held the makeshift knife to the crown of his head. Grimacing and with sappy tears running down his cheeks, he gouged and scraped until a good-sized strip of his pine scalp flitted through the air and settled on the dirt bed in the pot.

"Ouchie." He wiped his eyes on his forearm. Tote set the flower on the bit of scalp then filled in the dirt, pressing it down tight to support the broken stem.

"C'mon, my little friend," he whispered. He gave the side of the pot an encouraging tap-tap. "You can do it!"

He sat with his back to a tree and waited. Then, slowly but surely, the plant responded. A bit of green washed back to its leaves and the stem strained against itself like a hose trying to get unkinked.

Tote cheered the botanical phoenix on as it rose above the bucket rim, gradually returning to its full, abominable glory—something he had never seen before.

Tote felt like he had been hit by a tidal-wave of concentrated beauty and—drunk on it—he grabbed up the pot and took off running, looking for someone to show it to.

The sudden movement and the resulting bit of a breeze sent the blossoms' addictively awful aromas snaking through the trees. Cozy in its newfound freedom, the plant twitched a contented little twitch.

* * *

Tote ran through the night and most of the next morning, breathlessly telling the plant, in excruciating detail, what it was like to be unalive—making up stories about all the things that may or may not have been going on around him before he had the capacity to *know* what was going on around him.

He stopped suddenly, thrusting the plant in front of him. "I know! You need a name! Everything proper needs a name." He said, grinning his awful grin. "And finding a name could be a fun game!"

"Would you like to play a game, plant? I feel quite certain I like games, even having never played one. Do you know any name-games?"

He scratched his chin. "How about I start guessing names and you just—uh—do *something* when I'm getting close to one you like." Tote wasn't sure how but he had the distinct impression the plant *wanted* to play.

"So here we go. How about—hmm—Abe?" Tote waited a moment then frowned. "Abner? —Alfie? —Apple?"

* * *

Much, much later.

"Yarn? —Yakkie? Ya—" Tote was beginning to worry there weren't enough names left and that perhaps he had missed the signal, or skipped a name, when he felt warmth radiating from the pot.

"Ah ha! Yammer!" He shouted.

The pot got a smidge cooler.

* * *

Much, much later—again.

"Yottabecquerel!" Tote danced around, do-si-doing the pot—which had become so hot he had to switch it from hand to hand. "I can't believe I guessed that! And in only—uh—as many tries as I tried!"

"Quite a mouthful if you ask me, though. How about we shorten it up a bit?" He set the pot on a tree stump and began skipping in place. Skipping helped him think.

"Yot! Much easier to say," Tote slapped his knee, "and two times as good since *you* are in a *pot*. You-pot—Yot!"

Yot twitched.

* * *

The breeze whipped itself into a hearty gust pushing against Tote as he came up to the end of the forest. Ground-hugging grass and patchy spots of exposed stone went on a little ways and then just dropped off into nothingness. They had reached the end of the top of Mt. Illuso. Tote hadn't even realized they were on a mountain.

He had just come out of the sheltering forest when he discovered he wasn't alone.

A young Pineville girl was off a ways hurling rocks over the precipice with all her might. Tote ran back into the woods and hid behind a tree. He peeked out as the girl heaved a stone larger than her head into the void and perched on the edge like a gargoyle—watching it fall. Tote figured she must have been shouting pretty loud because her mouth was too open for talking and he thought he could hear the faintest whisper of a sound through his useless earhole. The girl looked very angry—her scrunched rosy face a stark contrast to her cheery yellow dress and shiny red locks—the hair painted so expertly it actually appeared to be blowing with the wind.

"*Crab apples!*" She shouted, rolling a stone too heavy to lift to the edge and nudging it over.

"I can't believe he asked that over-painted *puppet* to the spring jig instead of me." She kicked the dirt. "I like you *as a friend*, Beana," she said mockingly. "Sure, sure. What a coincidence that the girl you like *not as a friend* happens to have her dress carved short and painted on wood-tight."

Tote cringed in his hiding place. "Seems she could use some cheering up." He looked at Yot. "What do you think my leafy friend? Should we show her *true* beauty?"

He lurched out from behind the tree and started shambling in the direction of the girl. He didn't want to frighten her by coming up from behind at a top-speed skip.

Beana was just about to chuck another stony "he-loves-me-not" off the mountain when she saw Tote from the corner of her eye. The rock fell from her hand and her jaw dropped open.

When Beana realized the *thing* was looking at her—walking all weird up to her, waving some disgusting potted weed—she panicked and tried to get away, but stumbled over her pile of unpitched rocks. By the time she got herself together she realized she was in the deformed shadow of the whatever-it-was.

"Stay away!" She screamed, scooting back toward the sheer edge—boxed in by a deadly fall and a potentially deadly monster.

"Yes it *is* a stunning day, little miss. My name is—" Was all Tote got out before the girl darted by him and ran off into the woods.

Tote was confused. He had thought the sight of the most beautiful flower in the world would have cheered her up, not chased her off. Then he realized she was probably just running home to get all her friends so they too could witness the splendor of Yot. That must be it.

He decided to stay there until the cheering crowd of townsfolk came back, probably waving the shovels and hoes they would be using to build a grand monument for Yot.

Tote's Blemished Blossom

Tote pushed the stray rocks back into the pile with his toe then shimmied along the precipice and peeked over the edge of his known world.

"Yowzie!" He scrambled back a few steps. The drop-off was immediate and sheer. The flattish cliff-face plunged into a bed of bloated clouds—no visible ledges or changes in slope to break a fall.

"Wow, Yot! Would you take a look at *that*. I wonder what's down there."

Tote thought he could just make out a hushed sound—as if the clouds were calling out to him. He cupped his hand at his earhole and strained to hear what they might have to say. It sound like:

Die! You freak!

He turned and found himself face to tree branch as Beana introduced him to hers. She bashed again and again and with each hit Tote stumbled back a step. Then there were no more steps to stumble to.

He found himself teetering on the edge of the very edge of the mountain! He looked at the girl—down at the clouds—back at the girl. She sneered and poked him right between the eyes with the branch.

Tote hugged Yot close, curling around the plant and its pot as they fell.

* * *

How do?

Tote stood in the shadow of Yot, now taller than the sky—each blossom as big and breathtaking as a gilded fairy-tale palace. The voice, if it could be

called that, sounded like a whisper of wind blowing
between stamen spires.

"Um—hello?" Tote said.

Hullo?

"Yes—hello—" He shouted as loud as he could.
"Can you hear me now?"

Can you hear me?

Tote looked up the towering stalk of Yot—so large
the striations and textures formed ornate stairs and
hand-holds.

Tote's Blemished Blossom

"I can just barely hear you, Yot!" Tote pulled himself up on the first green ledge. "Let me get closer!"

I said, can you hear me? The voice was a bit louder now.

"I'm coming, Yot!" Tote scrambled up the stalk.

Hey Stickman!

Tote was about to inform Yot he didn't appreciate the nickname when a girthy tendril thrust out from the stalk, hit him squarely in the chest, and knocked him right off his little step. It was so sudden Tote didn't even have a chance to scream before he hit the ground with a *squish.*

A squish?

Anyone home?

Another shove, this time from some impolite poltergeist, submerged Tote in a thick goo. He came up sputtering and after wiping the sticky slime from his eyes he found himself at the base of a giant bush that was bending under the weight of tens of thousands of plump purple berries—so bloated and ripe they oozed from their stem-holes.

Making jam?

"Yot!" Tote jumped to his feet, fell face-first in the mound of smooshed berries, then belly-crawled until he was free of the branches and goo.

He found himself in the shadow of a hairy-faced giant wearing a dirty flannel shirt and dirtier coveralls. He was holding a rust-toothed saw in one hand

and, much to Tote's dismay, a rather dishevelled-looking, but still fabulous, Yot in the other.

The man's beard was moving whereabouts a mouth should be but Tote couldn't make out what he was saying. Whatever it was must have been funny though. The man nearly doubled over laughing.

Tote cleared the purple jelly from his ear-hole then licked his fingers. It was puckeringly sour but not unpleasant—kind of made his mouth tingly and alive.

He could faintly hear the man now—his guffaws deep, straight from the belly. Tote stood tall and proud as he could—what with the fact he only came up to the man's belt and looked like something a ghost with a sinus infection had coughed up.

Tote pointed at his pitiful excuse for an ear and said, "Sorry but I don't hear so well."

The man nodded then dug around the spot where his wild hair met up with the equally-wild sideburns and beard. He fished out an earlobe, tugged on it, then walked up to Tote and screamed in his face.

"I said you'll have to speak up! I'm hard of hearing—too much motosawing in a prior life!"

Now it was Tote's turn to laugh. He leaned in close to the man and shouted, "My ear isn't much good either!" He turned his head, displaying Dolly's amateurish oversight. "See what I mean?"

The man nodded again and the crinkles around his eyes suggested his reclusive mouth was grinning in the scraggly underbrush.

"It's mighty fortunate our voices are in tip-top shape!" The man shouted. "Else we'd spend the rest of the day standing around looking at each other!"

Tote smiled. "My name is Tote!" He extended his wooden hand, noted the berry-jam mittens he was wearing, and opted for a flourish and a bow instead.

The man tapped his stocking cap with the tip of his saw. "Raynaud Whitefinger," he said. "Preferably Whitefinger—EX-lumberman UN-extraordinaire!"

Whitefinger pointed up through the leafy canopy at the mountainside climbing into the clouds. "Thought you were another rock—they've been coming down on and off all day. Some pretty big ones too."

"Yeah—uh. I must have tripped." Tote was a bit uncomfortable about such close-talking—the need to shout directly in another person's face—but the brawny woodcutter didn't seem the least bit fazed.

"Quite a trip! If ya hadn't landed where ya did ya mighta wound up being in my campfire tonight— cooking me up a pot of steeped sap soup."

He switched Yot to his other arm, produced a dirty handkerchief from one of his many pockets, and draped it over Tote's shoulder. Tote gratefully started wiping himself off.

"So what's with the ugly flower?" Whitefinger said, holding Yot up to his ear. "That where your ears went? The little bugger talk 'em off?"

"*What?*" The kerchief fell to Tote's feet.

Tote's Blemished Blossom

"Started yammering about ten minutes ago—faintest whisper of a whisper but sure sounds like talkin' to me."

Without warning, the blossom nearest to Whitefinger's ear shriveled up and broke away from the stem.

* * *

Tote and Whitefinger walked side-by-side—the "woodsman" hunched over, the "wood-man" crane-necked and on tiptoes, and a very uncomfortable-looking potted plant pinned between their heads—the entire way to camp.

They made it a point to stop at every berry bush they came across. Tote said it was to be sure no other wood-men or glorious flowers had "fallen" off the mountain. The truth of the matter was that Tote had grown quite fond of the berries, popping them into his mouth by the handful at each bush they checked.

The men loudly exchanged their life stories in stunted bursts—pausing every few seconds to see if Yot had anything to add. Tote's life story didn't require many words and was cut even shorter since the second half of his life started right about when Tote woke up in the berry bush. Raynaud Whitefinger's story needed quite a bit more telling, though.

* * *

Raynaud was born and, yes, "raised" in a little town called Razington—where the men cut wood with huge mechanized saws, the women cooked cut-wood and oiled the monstrous metal wheels on their monstrous metal homes, and the youngins gnawed cooked-cut-wood with their nubby new teeth and stayed *away* from saw blades, boiling pots of pulp, and the monstrous metal wheels on monstrous metal homes.

Razington was easy to find but impossible to get directions to because the entire town was always moving—forever inching onward through untouched forest and leaving behind a continuous, flat surface of hardened wood-pulp in its wide wake.

One day, as the whining, ever-present grind of saws and dull cracking of trees filled the air, Raynaud Whitefinger decided he preferred not to cut trees.

His family was bewildered. Razington men *always* cut wood. They pleaded with him for days, even suggesting—with great reluctance—he try his hand at cooking cut-wood or keeping children from playing under the homes but he very adamantly preferred to not do those things either. Or much of anything for that matter. It wasn't long at all before Raynaud preferred to not inch onward through the woods along with the town. He stopped and stubbornly stood his ground as his family, friends, and life as he knew it left him—albeit very slowly and with ample time for a day of tearful pleading and the tossing of sacks of necessities and other things Raynaud's parents thought he would want.

Raynaud had been wandering aimlessly and camping without purpose ever since—settling down wherever he preferred to stop, and packing up when he preferred to move. One thing is for certain—Raynaud Whitefinger mostly preferred to not be bored but couldn't help being anything other than mostly bored most of the time.

* * *

The odd trio pushed through a patch of particularly thick undergrowth into Whitefinger's camp, which consisted of a pot over a pit of smouldering embers, three large canvas sacks bulging shapes and angles, a variety of saws, and a makeshift bed—canvas covering a pile of leaves.

Tote looked as if he'd *become* one of those plump berries—sticky-fingered, belly distended, and wood dyed a royal purple.

Whitefinger, apparently preferring to sleep, sprawled out on the leaf mattress and was snoring a woodcutter's snore moments later.

Tote gingerly placed an equally-exhausted, droopy-leafed Yot on a flat rock. Surprisingly, a tight green bud, hinting bright red at its seams, had popped up right where that other blossom had dropped off dead.

Tote felt a pang of discomfort in his belly—which was grumbling in time with the snoring pile of leaves. He sucked at each of his fingers searching for even a sliver of a stain of the purple berries he had developed quite a taste for.

Tote spied a berry bush through the trees and used a cooking-pot to forage quite an impressive pile of berries.

He slumped down next to Yot and whispered, "I don't know if that woodcutter really heard you talking but I do know—in my guts—you have something you need to tell *me*."

Then the little wood-man gorged himself to sleep and dreamt of talking flowers—and being shoved off a towering mountain of berries.

* * *

Over the next few days, Tote and Raynaud became more and more dedicated in their self-appointed quest to understand Yot—who became more and more agitated since each failed attempt cost it a blossom, and it clearly did not like losing those.

They tested every angle and location, even trying an alcove Whitefinger had carved in a tree trunk and lined with moss. They tried high above, amongst the gentle rustle of leaves in the breeze, and down low in the depths of a hole dug for that very purpose—where the only sounds were the mucousy slitherings of worms and the pit-pitting footfalls of industrious ants.

Tote finally heard *something* with a contraption they had created using items fished from Whitefinger's sacks—a sap-catcher funnel and a length of tubing that, when twisted just so, allowed the faintest of whispers to poke through the loud background noise of the forest. The woodsman was even more successful on that same device, claiming he heard something a hair louder than ever before. But it was still completely unintelligible.

Whitefinger dropped the funnel and kicked it clear across the camp. "I'm about ready to prefer we not do this any more," he said, angry resignation in his voice.

"Well I'm *never* giving up," Tote said. "Yot is the most wonderful creation in the whole wide world—and that most wonderful creation wants to talk to regular, lowly, old *me*."

Yot dropped another blossom and hunched over—leaves and petals limp with disheartenment.

Tote watched the metal funnel rolling back and forth—glinting in the sun. His head jerked up. He ran to Whitefinger, grabbed his bushy face, and screamed excitedly. "Do you know *why* the sap-catcher works better than anything else?"

"Well—" The woodsman's eyes wandered in thought. "The words must go in quiet on the wide end and come out loud on the small end—and if it works like sap then—"

"A cave!" Tote shouted. "Caves have *really* big open ends. Maybe if we put Yot at the entrance and go all the way to the back with our sound-catcher—"

"Hmm—" Whitefinger scratched at a slow grin spreading unseen beneath his beard. "Sounds like we'd better find ourselves a cave then."

Tote's belly grumbled. "*And* some more of those delectable berries!"

Guided only by the cool breeze at their backs, the unlikely trio set off through the woods in search of a cave. Tote carried a pail of berries in one hand and Yot—who had perked up considerably—tucked tight to his chest while Whitefinger had a sack of what he called "travel-sized necessities" slung over each shoulder.

* * *

A couple days later, the breeze that had been guiding them suddenly changed direction and blew a chill mist back in their faces. Soon enough they came to the base of a raging waterfall that neither of them had heard coming.

Knowing full well that any cave within a mile of there would only be gathering up the sound of crashing water, Tote and Whitefinger decided to follow the river downstream in the hopes it would simmer down and lead them to a nice, big-mouthed cave. And that's exactly what it did.

* * *

Tote stumbled upon, and would have stumbled *in* had his friend not stopped him, a hole in the ground so large and deep and dark it looked as if it could swallow an entire town—and may have done just that.

The monstrous hole quaffed the river like a man on his third day with no water. Tote marveled at how one moment they were strolling along the riverside and then all of a sudden the river was gone. Tote tossed a berry off the edge and shivered as the shadows gobbled it up.

Whitefinger saw a flash of bright orange on the far side—the *very* far side—of the hole and tapped Tote's shoulder to point it out to him. It looked like a huge, gangly bird flapping about with its plumage on full display. They started the long walk along the rocky rim for a closer look. Half-way around they realized it wasn't a spasmodic bird but rather an oddly-dressed man waving his arms excitedly and shouting soundlessly at them. He was wearing a violent clash of colors and styles that left him looking like a bunch of clowns whisked together. Nearby was a wheeled and canopied pull-cart brimming with wares as varied and random as his clothes.

"Ah, welcome fine travelers!" He barked as they drew up close. He gave an exaggerated bow. "Glucas, Trader of the Holes, at your service."

Whitefinger turned to Tote, who had stopped and was looking up at him questioningly. He bent down, cupped his hands over Tote's ear and said loudly, "He says he's got mucous and is a traitor to the moles!"

Glucas laughed and flicked the brim of his gaudy feathered hat. "Trouble communicating we have. Great care we must take for misunderstanding to avoid we not is—uh—"

He coughed so violently his arms windmilled, almost toppling him over into the gaping hole. He horked up something black and slimy and spat it into the abyss, then calmly walked over and slapped Whitefinger on the back.

"Sorry bout that," he screamed, pointing at his throat. "Post-nasal drip and so forth."

Glucas grabbed Whitefinger's fingers and pumped a handshake like he was drawing the last drops of water from a well. "My name is Glucas," he yelled directly in Whitefinger's face—spittle flying forth and losing itself

somewhere in the rat's nest of a beard. "Glucas—the one and definitely not only Trader of the Holes!"

Whitefinger looked at his hand furiously going up and down, still locked up, then back at the odd merchant. "I am Raynaud White—"

Glucas reeled back as though he had been punched in the face.

"Please sir," he wheezed, "*my* ears work just fine. So if you could speak a bit quieter that—" Glucas cocked his head as though listening to something. "Ah—hmm. Yes."

He fished around in one of a dozen pockets and pulled out a lump of beeswax. He divided it in half and stuffed a bit in each of his ears. "Customers are always right," he said, "and you two sure look like customers to me."

Glucas patted Tote on the head and looked at Whitefinger expectantly.

"Uhm, okay," the woodsman said uncertainly, "I am Ray—"

"You'll have to speak louder," the mixed-up salesman yelled, tugging on his own ears.

After a series of extremely loud introductions everyone felt adequately introduced and Glucas continued his spiel.

"So what are you fine travelers in need of?" He presented his cart with a flourish. It was so full of just about everything you could ever *not* need—as well as quite a few items whose function or purpose was a complete mystery.

"I have a bit of everything you may need, a lot of anything you don't need, but," he looked at his feet, moving the dirt and fallen leaves around with the heel of his bright yellow shoe and the toe of the shiny black one, "it pains me to say I am fresh out of nothing. It's on backorder—indefinitely."

Whitefinger and Tote nosed about the cart in curiosity. There were pots and pans, cots and fans, shovels, muzzles, and candied yams, cheese wheels, shoes with high heels, a toy boat, and what Tote was sure were the horns of a goat—just to name a few.

"Where did all this stuff come from?" Tote asked.

"Let's just say there are trucks—and sometimes things happen to fall off them."

"Trucks of fake plastic ducks?" Whitefinger asked skeptically.

"Best you not ask questions, my friend. Questions get my mojo out of whack. And when my mojo isn't just right my customers may be forced to walk away *without* exactly what they need." Glucas' eyes looked capable of boring holes to the brain then cutting a beeline to the wallet. "Simply *don't* ask questions and everyone walks away happy—albeit slightly confused."

"I don't think I need much of this stuff," Tote said, shaking a jar of hole-less buttons.

"Absurd!" Glucas said, shocked. "Why, you *need* anything and everything you don't *have* of course!"

Tote's Blemished Blossom

Whitefinger swung his two bulging sacks of necessities out for Glucas to see. "There's nothing we *need*. We were just searching for—"

"Ah, ah, ah. Then I can't help you, my friend. As I said, I'm fresh out of nothing."

Glucas turned to Tote—who was hugging Yot tight, still not too sure what to make of the situation.

"Ho, ho, I say! And what have we here?" Glucas yelled, noticing Yot for the first time. He grimaced and raised a bushy eyebrow. "I know what *you* need."

"Um, what *I* need?"

Glucas began frantically digging through his cart, flinging squarish wheels, butterfly nets, gravy ladles, muddy galoshes, and a number of other things into a motley pile on the ground. When he emerged he proudly displayed a pair of polished silver shears. In his other hand he had three large zebra-striped seeds.

"This will take care of that nasty weed problem," he snip-snipped the shears in demonstration, "and I also have a few *spectacular* sunflower seeds. Start one in the pot then move it to the ground and you'll have a flower tall enough to look your hairy friend here in the eye."

"Weed?" Tote jumped back out of the merchant's reach. "This most certainly is *not* a weed! Why, it's the most *splendiforous* thing that has ever popped up from the ground!"

Glucas snorted. "Splendiforous? That's the most—" He paused and cocked his head, then pinched the bridge of his nose and closed his eyes tight. "Riiiight. From this angle I have a better view and I—*must* agree—that's a, uh, breathtaking plant you have."

He tossed the shears and seeds over his shoulder and gave the gaping hole a long, hard look. "But you *could* put your weed in there—"

Tote was ready to defend Yot's honor by showing Glucas how the prodigal plant could speak but he certainly didn't want the words meant for him to be coming from such an unstylish, unappreciative buffoon. He shook his head.

"No? Yes! Of *course* it's a no. You thought I didn't already know that?" He vaulted from the wagon and advanced on Tote like a tiger stalking a lame wildebeest calf.

Tote felt a growing yet inexplicable desire to *make a deal.*

"Now I see! You've come to hock the weed—er—glorious flower, haven't you?" Glucas grinned. "Sell it, pawn it, collateralize it, broker a deal—yes, yes?"

Tote felt himself nodding against his will and reaching out for a handshake. His mouth started to form the word 'yes.'

Whitefinger stepped between them and crossed his arms, breaking the spell. Tote peeked out from behind Whitefinger's leg and screamed, "NO!" He shook his fist at Glucas. "Yot is *mine!* Mine and mine only! Stay back!"

Tote's Blemished Blossom

Whitefinger stepped aside and glared at Tote. "Um, I meant to say it's *ours*. Ours but nobody else." Tote's voice cracked.

"Eh, you saved me the trouble. I didn't want it anyway." Glucas seemed almost relieved.

Tote, an apparent anxious eater, popped the last few berries in his mouth and chewed away.

Glucas glanced at the empty bucket then at Tote. "Uh...how many of those have you eaten?"

Tote licked his fingers and smiled an uncomfortable, self-conscious smile. "What?"

"You *do* realize those are Muffleberries—" Glucas looked horrified.

Tote looked up at Whitefinger—equally dumbfounded—then shrugged. "What's a Muffleberry? Besides a dollop of heaven tastier than the sappiest sapsicle—"

"What's a *Muffleberry?*" Glucas gasped. He stepped to the rim of the giant black hole, cupped his hands over his mouth, and shouted, "Hear that? Woody here says 'what's a Muffleberry'."

Tote saw a rogue berry on the ground. He snatched it up and popped it in his mouth.

Glucas winced. Then in a very unsalesman-like voice he said, "How 'bout you sit your pine butt down there and I'll tell you a little story about Muffleberries."

* * *

"Once, long ago, there was a young boy named Timmy. Actually, there are probably many Timmys in a variety of times ago but for this tale it's just the one at just the right time—long ago.

This exact Timmy loved to dream. In his village he was known for blank-faced, one-sided conversations and his klutzy habit of walking into poles, tripping over stones, and falling down the well.

Each time Timmy was rescued from the well his exasperated family would ask, "*What* were you thinking?!"

And his reply, in the rare times he wasn't too mentally preoccupied to give one, was always, "Not much—just thinking."

Timmy, of course, was lying.

In his mind the boy was invariably on a grand adventure—slaying dragons, swimming the depths of the ocean, or climbing a tree that reached the stars. He would meet novel characters, face insurmountable obstacles, surmount surmountable mounts, and battle a variety of very villainous villains.

Timmy's thoughts contained the souls of stories— some of the greatest stories never told. For Timmy *never* told his stories. He kept them locked away in the prison of his mind and only allowed them out of their cells for parole hearings—Warden Timmy *never* granted parole.

One day, he was so consumed by a tale—one so unlike anything he'd ever concocted—he was unaware that at least a dozen villagers had individually confronted him—each dying to know what was so interesting and why he couldn't spare a moment or even a "just thinking."

Tote's Blemished Blossom

Timmy was so focused on the story he didn't notice he had wandered away from the village. And he certainly had no idea when he passed the farthest point any villager ever dared to go, unwittingly plunging into the great unknown of the woods.

He walked and walked, oblivious to the musical rustle of foreign leaves, the rush and flow of a nameless river, and the chittering of odd forest creatures he'd never encountered before. Then, in true form, Timmy fell down a hole. It was a big hole. And it was a big fall.

When he awoke he found himself in a damp, chilled darkness that was so thick he couldn't even see the stream lazily gurgling right beside him. Luckily, years of sightless wandering around town had prepared him for this very moment. In no time at all Timmy felt comfortable enough navigating the labyrinthine cave passages to pick up the story where he left off after having been so rudely interrupted by unconsciousness.

Much later, Timmy's tale was again interrupted—this time by the slick, wet wall marking the end of the cave.

(If Tote had ears they would have perked up at the mention of cave endings. He leaned in so close to Glucas he was shaded by the merchant's wide-brimmed hat.)

The distracted boy also felt the workings of another inevitable interruption—his belly was grumbling something fierce and he doubted stalactites and mites would satiate it.

Just then, Timmy's internal rumblings seemed to become the epicenter of a much greater rumbling—an earthquake that shook the cave like a child shaking a wrapped present trying guess what's inside. He bounced about on the ground a bit and when everything other than his stomach settled down he noticed the cave wasn't pitch black any more.

There was now a sliver of light far, far overhead. And through that tiny, new gap fell a plump, ripe berry. It was what we now know—what *some* of us now know—is a Muffleberry. Timmy popped it in his mouth and then, just as he finished chewing up the thick, sour skin, another berry fell. Then another. And another.

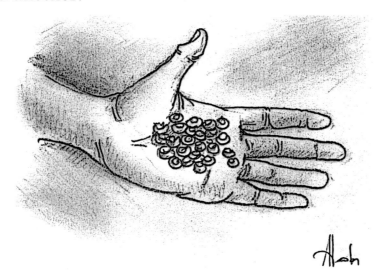

The seemingly endless supply of berries and the steady trickle of water was just enough sustenance for Timmy to focus his full attention on the stories locked up in his mind. And so that's exactly what he did.

Big changes often go unnoticed when they are the result of lots and lots of little changes over time. Timmy didn't realize his head was growing until it became too heavy to lift and he was forced to log-roll just for a drink of water. When his arms were no longer long enough to reach past his chin he had to position his head in just the right way so the falling berries would land directly in his mouth.

That's about when the Muffleberries started earning their namesake. As Timmy's surroundings were muffled, becoming *less* his surroundings, his thoughts got louder, bolder, and bigger—as did the need to contain them. Fueled by berries, his head kept growing and his skull became as thick and hard as the very walls of the cave itself.

Fortunately, it grew right up to that sliver of light in the ceiling and completely uprooted the patch of Muffleberries, cutting off his supply. The growth stopped but Timmy's ideas didn't, and, unable to penetrate the thick bone walls, they eventually filled up his head until there wasn't any room left, forcing him to think the same thoughts over and over.

Timmy, of course, got bored. And over time he *forgot* how to come up with ideas. Then he started forgetting the ideas he already had. He had muffled everything outside his head and forgotten everything inside it and right now, at this very moment, that little boy is *still* trapped—bored out of his mind *in* his mind.

Moral of the story? Don't eat the flabobbin' Muffleberries!

If that kid had kept eating, his prison of a head may have grown big as the *entire* Land of Ev and

perhaps I would be telling this story inside his brain instead of outside it."

* * *

"And how exactly do you know all this?" Whitefinger asked.

Glucas looked back at the hole and cringed. "Not a question you should be asking, my friend."

Whitefinger was having none of that. "Just answer the ques—"

"So you're saying I'll turn into a *cave* just by eating little purple berries?" Tote interrupted, his belly grumbling.

Glucas looked relieved. He wiped a trickle of sweat from his brow. "Cave? No, no, not at all. The berries amplify who you *really* are by quieting down all the stuff you definitely aren't—and the stuff you think you want to be—and the stuff you think you are."

He looked at the empty pail at Tote's feet. "Luckily you'd have to eat a LOT of them to cause any real trouble. One bucket *probably* won't—"

Whitefinger cleared his throat and mumbled, "It wasn't just the one."

"What?"

Whitefinger looked regretfully at Tote. "I said that bunch of, uh, Muffleberries wasn't the first."

Eye's wide, Glucas inched behind the cart. His voice quavered. "It pains me to say—*truly* pains me—that you may *prefer* to take your business elsewhere and—"

"*But*," Whitefinger said firmly, "I personally witnessed him eat his first berry and we just watched him eat his last. That wood noggin is odd enough as it is. *Big* odd we'd surely notice."

Glucas nervously flicked flecks of red paint from the wagon handles. He cocked his head again and was again sedated by *something*.

"Yes, yes," he said, moving in close to the two travelers. "*Immunity*, my friends. Perhaps talking logs are *immune*." He knocked on the top of Tote's head like it was a door. "Back to business then. Weren't you just saying you needed—?"

"I was saying I would prefer not to buy anything."

"Not anything? But—"

"Nothing," Whitefinger said.

"Bah." Glucas pressed a hidden button on his cart and a false panel on the side dropped open, revealing stacks of clothing, mugs, unusual water-balls that each had a tiny version of Glucas and his cart inside, spatulas inscribed with the phrase, 'Went to Glucas the Hole Trader and all I got was this stupid spatula,' and a variety of other items stamped with the GG logo. "How about some Glucas-Gear then?"

Tote, appearing to be in some sort of trance, started shambling toward the cart but Whitefinger quickly grabbed his shoulder.

"Not a chance," he said. He picked up the pail, stuffed it in one of his sacks, and started leading Tote away. "And now I think we'll *prefer* to be on our way again. Caves don't find themselves."

"But look!" Glucas cried in desperation as he furiously bopped an official Glucas-Gear paddle-ball. He grabbed a GG whistle from a basket full of them and held it high. "Look! Look! You *need* this!"

Whitefinger waved back without turning. "I would prefer not to look!"

"Wait!" Glucas ran after them and hurled himself in front of Whitefinger, colliding firmly but not slowing the big man down at all. "At least a handshake," he said, pleading. "You can't leave a business deal with no handshake!"

"There was no deal—so no handshake," Whitefinger said, continuing on his way with Tote at his side.

"But–" Tote murmured, trying desperately to slip away to see the new merchandise. Whitefinger kicked the little wood-man's little wood-rear and then the two marched off into the forest.

* * *

For days they searched for a cave and for days they found nothing. Every so often Whitefinger would tinker with his sap-catcher hearing aid and Yot would drop another withered blossom in frustration. Tote, on the other hand, was battling a different problem— one he was pretty sure his friend should never find out about.

Each night, when Whitefinger was asleep, Tote would unhook his pail from the campfire, slip the sound-funnel from its sack, and slink off into the woods with Yot. He was determined to hear what Yot was saying—and to hear it first. Which is one reason he was keeping his nocturnal activities a secret. The other reason was that his plan required the mass consumption of Muffleberries. And while that was, in his mind, the most delicious perk a secret plan ever had, he was pretty sure the woodsman would not be happy about it. Not in the least.

This is why Tote was more than a little frightened when Whitefinger burst forth from the darkness one night.

"Aha!" Whitefinger shouted.

Tote would have made some exclamation of surprise had his mouth not been stuffed full of Muffleberries. Even Yot appeared a bit startled—its stems recoiling and leaves shaking.

"So *this* is where you've been sneaking off to every night."

Tote wiped sticky berry remnants from his chin and nodded, unsure of what he could say that wouldn't make him out to be a horribly selfish person.

"It's, uh, not what it looks like."

"So I *didn't* just catch my friend gorging himself on the one thing he promised to never eat again?"

"Well, when you put it that way—" Tote plucked the sap-catcher tube from his ear-hole and held it up. "I meant *this* probably looks like I'm trying to hear Yot first and maybe—not tell you about it?"

Whitefinger crossed his arms.

Tote hung his head low. "Well—maybe it is what it looks like—but just a little." He looked up at the angry log-chopping Santa towering over him. "I was going to tell you. *Really.* I just wanted it to be a surprise," he paused, "but mostly I didn't want you to know I was on the berries again."

Tote's Blemished Blossom

The tumultuous activity in Whitefinger's facial hair gradually subsided. He sat down heavily on the ground next to Tote.

"So does it work?" He asked.

"Huh?"

"The berries—are they doing anything? Your head doesn't seem any bigger and you're just as ugly as ever."

Tote didn't feel it was an appropriate time to defend his appearance. He placed the hearing tube on his friend's thigh. "I'm not really sure. It *seems* like it might be a little better but I can only hear about half as well as you I think."

Whitefinger stuck the tube in his ear and tapped Yot's pot. As always, he could hear *something* being said—he just wasn't sure what. But for the first time since hitting puberty the woodcutter's mouth was visible—primarily because it was hanging open about as far as it could go.

"What?!" Tote jumped up—a curious mix of excitement, jealousy, and disappointment in his voice. "Did you hear something? Did you? What did it say?"

"It's not what I heard," Whitefinger said, his eyes wild with new hope, "it's what I *didn't* hear!"

"You know how our hearing tube picks up and amplifies *all* the forest noise—buzzing beetles, blown leaves, chirpy birds, and such?" Whitefinger held Tote's shoulders and was yelling right in his face.

Tote nodded, unsure of where this outburst had come from, or where it was going.

"Well," the woodsman said trembling, "that obnoxious cacophony wasn't as obnoxious. In fact, some of the typical sounds weren't there at all!"

"Sooo," Tote was a bit confused, "it's a *good* thing that we can't hear other sounds in addition to not being able to hear Yot?"

Whitefinger snapped his fingers, then grabbed the sap-catcher hearing aid and Yot in its pot. "Stay here! I'll be back," he shouted as he ran off into the woods.

So Tote stayed and stayed and was beginning to worry he'd been duped and that Whitefinger was giving him a taste of his own spoiled sap by running off like that—trying to be the first to hear Yot actually speak. But Whitefinger did come back. As the morning sun broke over the trees, Raynaud Whitefinger walked out from the dwindling shadows, dragging behind him the hearing aid by the end of its long tube, the giant funnel skittering along a ways behind as it hit small rocks and bits of rotted wood. Yot was dangling loosely in his other hand.

The woodcutter's face was grey-white instead of the usual ruddy brown that comes from a life lived outdoors. And, even though almost completely masked by the beard, Tote could see some new type of expression was going on in there—a collision of joy and melancholy, excitement and serious concern.

Whitefinger sat down next to Tote and put his arm around the little pine man. "It's you," he said.

Tote looked at him questioningly.

Whitefinger pointed at a stray Muffleberry. "And those."

Tote's Blemished Blossom

Through careful, tedious experimentation, Whitefinger hypothesized that the Muffleberries had created some sort of 'dome of quiet' around Tote. And eating more berries seemed to be making the dome bigger, dampening the already quieted sounds nearby as well as the louder sounds drifting in from farther away.

As the bubble grew, Whitefinger and Tote could hear each other and the whisperings of Yot a little better. They felt the time was nearly at hand—the monumental moment when they could *truly* hear what had seemed destined to remain unheard.

* * *

Whitefinger set another bucket of berries by Tote's feet. "That's forty-six," he said. "Hopefully our magic number."

Tote wore a puff-cheeked smile but it went unseen, buried—like every other part of his body—under a half-inch thick layer of Muffleberry slime. "Hhmpuly," he said, jawing like a cow.

The woodsman returned Yot to his rightful throne atop the stump of a tree that had given itself to the saw-blade and the continued glow of the campfire. Whitefinger pulled his kerchief, squatted next to Tote and wiped the wood-man's brow. He leaned in close and squinted, inspecting the spot he had just cleaned, then jerked his head back in panic.

"Spit it out!" He screamed.

"Hhmph?"

Whitefinger slapped the back of Tote's head—hard. "Spit it *out*, I said!" He started frantically scrubbing berry slop from Tote's arms like he was cleaning up evidence of some horrible crime.

Tote whimpered and let the well-chewed goo ooze from his mouth and down his chin, where it was immediately wiped away in a kerchief flurry. Shivering, he let himself be subjected to the sudden and violent spring cleaning.

Tote figured they had been at it too long and the constant failures had made Whitefinger prefer to be a raving lunatic instead of his friend. Or, Tote thought, maybe he just discovered Yot was speaking gibberish...

"Stupid, stupid, stupid!" Whitefinger hit himself on the thigh—winding up and coming down so hard it looked like he was trying to chop his leg off just like he chopped wood.

Then the woodsman put his head in his hands and cried, repeating "I'm sorry," over and over between choking sobs.

Whitefinger suddenly stood up and loomed over Tote like a storm cloud. "We're done!" He yelled— eyes all red and puffy.

"Done—?"

"Done with *all* this!" Whitefinger waived his hand at pretty much the entire camp—maybe the whole world. "Berries and funnels and especially," he glared in the direction of Yot, "*stupid* mumbling plants!"

"But I don't—"

Whitefinger grabbed Tote's arm, yanked it up, and shoved it in his startled face. "Look at yourself!"

Tote's Blemished Blossom

Tote flinched—eyes closed tight.

"I said look!"

Tote opened his eyes and looked at his hand—or *through* it rather.

* * *

They had made great progress in the Muffleberry plan but this current setback was crippling. Tote argued that he didn't feel any different and he knew in his pithy gut that it would only take a couple more buckets before they succeeded.

Whitefinger counterclaimed that it wasn't worth the risk of Tote vanishing, and they had already gone too far, and what if the bubble of quiet didn't stop growing and eventually covered the whole land of Ev?

He went so far as to say that maybe all this effort wasn't worth it anyway. What if Yot just wanted small-talk—the weather, and trite how-are-you-doings?

Tote and Whitefinger went at it for days—arguing, proposing new versions of failed plans, and discussing the forbidden idea that perhaps someone else—someone with fully functional hearing—should be the one to first hear Yot—maybe *ever* hear Yot.

But just as things seemed to be coming to a head, the camp calmed down. This was because Whitefinger was figuring out how to tell his closest and only friend that he preferred they part ways.

The confrontations also ceased because Tote, the defective, extraordinarily ordinary wooden man, had secretly constructed a device to concentrate and distill Muffleberries.

And it worked.

* * *

Tote sat with his back against a tree trunk, neck craned to see the bright stars poking holes in the crisp black night, which in turn punched holes in the lighter black of the shifting canopy—a sea of shadowed leaves.

The tiny acorn in his hand was bumpy and discolored—not even very acornish—but it was the culmination of all Tote's work. He carefully lifted the top off and looked at the nearly glowing purple gel inside the hollowed-out shell. There was barely enough to fill a thimble. But this was it.

* * *

Raynaud Whitefinger made use of his window of opportunity and gathered his belongings, cinching his sacks tight and piling them at the edge of camp. He looked over at Yot—its disfigured red blossoms dancing as the flickering fire played with shadow and light across its leaves. Yot was lucky the woodsman wasn't acting on all his preferences tonight because he really, really preferred to toss the twisted, teasing, taunting plant—pot and all—on the fire just to see its unheard words burn.

Whitefinger sighed, wondering how long it took for wooden men to go to the bathroom—especially considering he was reasonably sure wooden men *couldn't* go to the bathroom—let alone *have to*. Heck, he himself had been traipsing around the woods for years and never once went to the bathroom. But maybe that was just because he preferred not to.

Whitefinger yawned and decided to take a short nap while he waited.

Tote's Blemished Blossom

* * *

Tote was no good with numbers but he figured his odds anyway:

A 50% chance it would make him just a tad more invisible and work well enough for him to hear Yot.

A 25% chance it wouldn't do anything.

A 30% chance it would do bad things.

And a 5% chance it would do *really* bad things.

He shuddered, hoping "I have to go to the bathroom" wouldn't wind up being his Last Words.

But he knew in his heart it was all worth it, regardless of whether he became invisible—or *gone*. At least Whitefinger would still be there and hopefully *he* would be able to hear Yot.

Tote raised the acorn in a toast. "Well, here's to hearing!"

He popped it in his mouth, took a deep breath, closed his eyes, and bit down. The shell cracked, squirting sour warmth down his throat.

Tote felt odd—then he felt nothing.

His second set of last words wound up being much more memorable than the first. It's unfortunate no one was around to hear them.

* * *

The next morning, when Raynaud Whitefinger realized he had over-napped, and that Tote was gone, he figured it was another of the wood-man's attempts to hear Yot's first hearable words. But Yot was still there, sitting on its tree-stump throne—waiting.

Whitefinger searched around camp but found nothing—not a scrap of evidence that Tote had left temporarily, let alone permanently.

He grabbed the coiled-up hearing aid and set off into the woods, expanding his search until he reached its end in every direction.

Tote was nowhere to be found but Whitefinger discovered that the dome of quiet now covered the *entire* forest—from the mountains marking one side to the plains marking the other. With tears in his eyes, he came to realize what Tote had done—and what he must do as well.

Back at camp, Whitefinger flopped down next to Yot and held the sap-catcher up to the quivering plant. He carefully slipped the earpiece in then knocked on Yot's pot and listened.

The spent blossom dropped off.

Whitefinger slowly pulled the tube from his ear. He stood up, his whole body tensed, his hand gripping the tube so tight his knuckles were white.

Everything had worked out—almost.

As he listened he got fragments of *actual* words here and there but they were all interrupted by bird tweets and incorrectly punctuated by distant deer stomping their hooves on the ground. He was—so close. And now Tote was gone.

* * *

Whitefinger swung the hearing aid around like a grappling hook and threw it up in a tree. He stomped

around camp hurling items from his bags into the woods and stringing together such a plentitude of vile, disgusting, taboo, depraved curses and swears that ears burned from the forest to the farthest reaches of Ev.

The raging woodsman picked up the trembling Yot and yanked it from its pot. Dirt clumps fell away, leaving the red roots naked and tangled.

Whitefinger slow-danced circles around the fire, snapping Yot's roots one by one. He was so consumed by vengeance he failed to see the hole—some burrowing mammal's doorstep partly hidden by fallen leaves.

His foot sunk in past the ankle and he came crashing down. While rolling on the ground, attempting to get up, Whitefinger felt a pointy lump in one of the pockets he had always preferred not to use.

It was a whistle—cheaply carved from pine and embossed with the letters "G.G." Whitefinger put it in his mouth, puffed up his cheeks and blew as hard as he could.

Nothing. The whistle made no sound.

What Whitefinger did notice, however, was that an angry mockingbird—who had flitted down to find out who had almost clobbered it with a sap-catcher—jerked as if it had been hit with a rock. When the woodsman blew the whistle again the bird convulsed a moment then flew away in a panic—far, far away.

Whitefinger had to go quite a ways out of camp to even find another bird to experiment on. He spotted a cardinal, blew the whistle, and—like before— the stunned bird flew off. A family of squirrels also bolted from their nest nearby and scampered through the woods.

He continued to blow as he walked around the forest and wherever he went all sorts of life, from birds and bears down to the lowliest beetle, fled as if the forest was on fire.

Baffled, but admittedly having a bit of fun, Whitefinger blew the whistle the whole time he marched back to camp.

When he saw the battered Yot half-dead on the ground, he felt a twang of guilt. Everything Tote had lived for—and unlived for—was in those snapped roots and awkwardly splayed leaves, the bent stem, and the mashed blossoms. The whistle was an unexpected variable and he owed it to Tote to test it.

He set Yot back in its pot and packed it with dirt. Then he threw rocks at the sap-catcher until one caught the rim of the funnel and knocked it out of the tree. He propped it in front of the sorry-looking plant and slid the tube in his ear.

Silence.

One of the flowers twitched a bit and turned toward the funnel.

Then Yot *spoke*. And Whitefinger *heard*.

In a weak, child-like voice, Yot's blossom said:

I sure hope you have a pen or pencil.

OZ BIBLIOGRAPHY

Original Oz Canon [40 Books]

L. Frank Baum [14 Books]

1---The Wonderful Wizard of Oz (illus. W.W. Denslow)(1900)
2---The Marvelous Land of Oz (illus. John R. Neill)(1904)
3---Ozma of Oz (illus. John R. Neill)(1907)
4---Dorothy and the Wizard in Oz (illus. John R. Neill)(1908)
5---The Road to Oz (illus. John R. Neill)(1909)
6---The Emerald City of Oz (illus. John R. Neill)(1910)
7---The Patchwork Girl of Oz (illus. John R. Neill)(1913)
8---Tik-Tok of Oz (illus. John R. Neill)(1914)
9---The Scarecrow of Oz (illus. John R. Neill)(1915)
10--Rinkitink in Oz (illus. John R. Neill)(1916)
11--The Lost Princess of Oz (illus. John R. Neill)(1917)
12--The Tin Woodman of Oz (illus. John R. Neill)(1918)
13--The Magic of Oz (illus. John R. Neill)(1919)
14--Glinda of Oz (illus. John R. Neill)(1920)

Ruth Plumly Thompson [19 Books]

15--The Royal Book of Oz (illus. John R. Neill)(1921)
16--Kabumpo in Oz (illus. John R. Neill)(1922)
17--The Cowardly Lion of Oz (illus. John R. Neill)(1923)
18--Grampa in Oz (illus. John R. Neill)(1924)
19--The Lost King of Oz (illus. John R. Neill)(1925)
20--The Hungry Tiger of Oz (illus. John R. Neill)(1926)
21--The Gnome King of Oz (illus. John R. Neill)(1927)
22--The Giant Horse of Oz (illus. John R. Neill)(1928)

23--Jack Pumpkinhead of Oz (illus. John R. Neill)(1929)

24--The Yellow Knight of Oz (illus. John R. Neill)(1930)

25--Pirates in Oz (illus. John R. Neill)(1931)

26--The Purple Prince of Oz (illus. John R. Neill)(1932)

27--Ojo in Oz (illus. John R. Neill)(1933)

28--Speedy in Oz (illus. John R. Neill)(1934)

29--The Wishing Horse of Oz (illus. John R. Neill)(1935)

30--Captain Salt in Oz (illus. John R. Neill)(1936)

31--Handy Mandy in Oz (illus. John R. Neill)(1937)

32--The Silver Princess in Oz (illus. John R. Neill)(1938)

33--Ozoplaning with the Wizard of OZ (illus. John R. Neill)(1939)

John R. Neill [3 Books]

34--The Wonder City of Oz (illus. John R. Neill)(1940)

35--The Scalawagons of Oz (illus. John R. Neill)(1941)

36--Lucky Bucky in Oz (illus. John R. Neill)(1942)

Jack Snow [2 Books]

37--The Magical Mimics in Oz (illus. Frank Kramer)(1946)

38--The Shaggy Man of Oz (illus. Frank Kramer)(1949)

Rachel R. Cosgrove [1 Book]

39--The Hidden Valley of Oz (illus. Dirk Gringhuis)(1951)

Eloise Jarvis McGraw and Lauren Lynn McGraw [1 Book]

40--Merry Go Round in Oz (illus. Dick Martin)(1963)

Extension of Canon - (Authorized by Baum family)[4 Books]

Sherwood Smith [2 Books + 2 TBA]

41--The Emerald Wand of Oz (illus. William Stout)(2005)
42--Trouble Under Oz (illus. William Stout)(2006)
43--TBA (unknown)(unknown)
44--TBA (unknown)(unknown)

Empty-Grave Editions

Adam Nicolai [3 Short Stories] Retrofit Editions

32--The Silver Princess in Oz (February 2012)
> including *Gludwig and the Red Hair* (illus. Ardian Hoda)

38--The Shaggy Man of Oz (March 2012)
> including *Ruprecht the Castaway King* (illus. Ardian Hoda)

37--The Magical Mimics in Oz (May 2012)
> including *Tote's Blemished Blossom* (illus. Ardian Hoda)

Adam Nicolai [2 Books] Original Release

N0--The Tales of Yot (Summer 2012)
N1--Asper and the Unheard Heroes in Oz (1st Quarter 2013)

Empty-Grave Publishing

2012 is the Year of All Things Oz

The Silver Princess in Oz

The Shaggy Man of Oz (1st Quarter)

The Magical Mimics in Oz (2nd Quarter)

The Tales of Yot (2nd Quarter)

Asper and the Unheard Heroes in Oz (Early 2013)

Keep track of the happenings at:

oz.empty-grave.com

CPSIA information can be obtained
at www.ICGtesting.com
Printed in the USA
FFOW04n0931221115
18894FF